FINDING
MR RIGHT
IN FLORENCE

FINDING MR RIGHT IN FLORENCE

KATE HARDY

MILLS & BOON

First published in Great Britain 2019
by Mills & Boon, an imprint of HarperCollins*Publishers*
1 London Bridge Street, London, SE1 9GF

Large Print edition 2019

© 2019 Pamela Brooks

ISBN: 978-0-263-08268-5

MIX
Paper from
responsible sources
FSC www.fsc.org   FSC® C007454

This book is produced from independently certified FSC™ paper to ensure responsible forest management. For more information visit www.harpercollins.co.uk/green.

Printed and bound in Great Britain
by CPI Group (UK) Ltd, Croydon, CR0 4YY

For Gerard, who shared
the wonders of Florence with me.

CHAPTER ONE

Mariana Thackeray.

Angelo Beresford looked at the name on the email his sister had sent him.

Mariana was a presenter on a television programme about art—about paintings people had found in their attic or had been hanging on a wall unremarked-on for years, and then they turned out to be lost masterpieces worth a small fortune.

Camilla had spent the last couple of months of her pregnancy making a special trip from Rome to Florence every week to watch the programme with their grandfather. And Leo Moretti had apparently taken a real shine to the woman. He called her the Debussy girl—the girl with the flaxen hair. Cammie's version was that she looked like a pre-Raphaelite model.

Though it didn't matter what Mariana Thackeray looked like. What Angelo wanted from her had nothing to do with her looks and everything to do with what was inside her head.

Did Mariana Thackeray really know her stuff about art, or was she presenting the programme from a script?

There was only one way to find out.

Angelo flicked into the Internet and typed in the programme's name.

Her profile came up on the programme's website, along with a couple of links to newspaper articles.

Yup. She looked exactly like a model for one of his grandfather's nineteenth-century paintings. Long golden curls, blue eyes, fine cheekbones, and a sensual curve to her mouth. She was absolutely gorgeous.

He shook himself. That wasn't what he needed to know.

He looked at the caption. *Mariana Thackeray, MA. Broadcaster and art historian.*

Solid academic qualifications: she worked from knowledge rather than just a script, then. Good.

And the next bit was better still: she was

studying Italian nineteenth-century art for her PhD. His grandfather's passion. So she'd be just about the perfect person to help Angelo achieve his aims.

He wanted to check out her TV programme first, though. According to the Internet TV guides, it wasn't on air or even on catch-up TV at the moment; though a new series was planned for October.

Right now it was May. So, although Angelo didn't know exactly what the lead time of her series was, there was a good chance that she'd have the time to do the work he needed her to do. Better and better. The ducks were lining up nicely in a row.

The programme trailers were available, but a couple of minutes of screen time weren't really enough to tell him what he wanted to know. He went in search of the full episodes, guessing that someone would have downloaded them to the Internet, and bookmarked them in his laptop for viewing later that evening. Then he checked out the newspaper articles.

It looked as if her former partner was a nasty piece of work, a bully who was quite happy to lie in court and who'd made her life miserable in the extreme. Although Angelo's own branch of law was a very different one, he had friends who worked in that area and he knew how gruelling a case like that could be.

Mariana Thackeray had enough strength of character to stand up for herself in court and tell the truth, even though it must've been painful for her to have her life laid bare before strangers and scrutinised, and she'd spoken out in the newspaper article about how it felt to be in an abusive relationship and where you could get help. She'd talked about how easy it was to doubt yourself and think that the rows were all your fault. How easy it was to believe that you were useless and unworthy, drip by slow drip; how it felt to question your own reality and feel guilty that you were doubting your partner.

And she'd been frank about how hard it was to build yourself up again, how counselling could help you shift your mindset. She'd used her own painful experiences to help others. And the journalist had made it very clear that Mariana's fee for the interview had been donated to a women's refuge. He liked that: she hadn't profited from the experience, but used it to help others.

On one hand, it was a complication he could do without—a nasty-tempered ex who might want to make trouble. On the other, Angelo respected the fact that Mariana hadn't let the experience drag her down. That she'd worked hard and gone on to make a good life for herself, built herself back up from nothing.

He'd check out the programme, and then he'd make the decision about whether to contact her.

When he finally got home, Angelo ended up watching four episodes of *Hidden Treasure* back-to-back.

Now he knew exactly what had caught his grandfather's attention: Mariana's passion for art. Yes, she was beautiful. But it was when she talked about art that she really came alive. She *sparkled*. She took her audience along with her, showing them the technical side of the paintings and how the brushstrokes and pigments could be analysed; and she brought in the human side, showing snippets of the painter's life and where that particular painting fitted in. But most of all she brought out what the painting meant to the owner.

None of it seemed to be about the money. It was about vindication. Proving that the owners weren't dreaming about the art they'd fallen in love with—that they had a genuine painting rather than a copy or a fake. Something that could be traced all the way back to the artist; even when there wasn't a traditional paper trail, there were other bits of evidence that could back up a hunch. Scientific evidence.

Vindication.

That was what Angelo's grandfather needed. Proof that the painting he'd loved for years, his pride and joy, really was a Carulli. *The Girl in the Window.*

If anyone could prove it, Mariana Thackeray could. Even if it wasn't a suitable candidate for the show, he could still commission her to investigate the painting privately. He was perfectly happy to pay; what was the point in having money in the bank when you could use it to help someone you loved?

Angelo flicked into the word-processing program on his laptop and began to write.

* * *

The last lead in the file was a letter.

Most of the correspondence to *Hidden Treasure*, the television programme Mariana presented about lost art treasures found in people's homes, came by email, and she'd already sifted through this week's batch to find three potential leads for further investigation and sent a standard reply to the rest, thanking them for their interest and apologising that unfortunately they weren't suitable for the programme but she wished them the very best.

Letters were rare.

This one was from a lawyer, Angelo Beresford, requesting her to call him and set up a meeting to discuss a painting. Two words leaped out at her immediately: Domenico Carulli.

The main painter out of the group of artists she was studying for her PhD.

Intrigued, she flicked into the Internet to check out the firm of solicitors on the headed paper. Their website listed Angelo Beresford as a mergers and acquisitions specialist. So why was he writing to *Hidden Treasure*? Did a company he was working with think they had a painting worth a considerable amount of money and he wanted her professional opinion?

She didn't get involved in artwork valuation as a rule. Half her time was spent on her studies, and the other half in detective work for the television programme.

But.

Domenico Carulli.

Her favourite painter.

Angelo Beresford hadn't said which painting it was, and most of the ones she knew about were in a handful of galleries; there were a few in private hands, but none that she knew of in a corporate collection. Which could mean this was the kind of painting she looked at on *Hidden Treasure*. One that had gone unremarked and forgotten about for years. The lead was definitely worth checking out.

She picked up the phone and called his number.

'Mr Beresford's secretary,' a plummy voice announced.

'May I speak to Mr Beresford, please?' Mariana asked.

'I'm afraid he's in a meeting. May I take a message?'

'Thank you. My name's Mariana Thackeray. He wrote to me saying—'

'—that he wants to discuss a painting. Yes,' his secretary confirmed. 'He was hoping that you'd call. I have his diary in front of me. Would you like me to book an appointment?'

'Couldn't I just talk to him on the phone?' Mariana asked.

'I think he would prefer a face to face meeting with you, Miss Thackeray.'

Did that mean Angelo Beresford actually had the painting in his office and wanted her to take a look at it? All the hairs on her neck stood up in a rush of adrenaline. 'All right. When do you suggest?'

'He's free at half past two today,' the secretary said.

It would mean moving her meeting with Nigel, her producer, but if her hunch checked out then she was sure Nigel wouldn't mind. 'All right. Can I confirm the address?' She read out the address from the top of the letter.

'That's correct, Miss Thackeray. We'll see you at half past two.'

'Thank you for your help.' She ended the call and rang Nigel.

'Sweetie, I'm running late. Can we talk about it in our meeting this afternoon?' he asked.

'That's why I'm calling. I need to move our meeting because I'm chasing up a lead.'

'I'm about to go into another meeting,' he warned. 'I can give you thirty seconds.'

'OK. I've been through this week's mail. Three possibles, lots of sorry-not-for-us-es, and a letter about what I think is an unknown Carulli. A lawyer wants to see me about it this afternoon. So can I see you on Monday morning instead?'

Nigel groaned. 'I *hate* Monday mornings.'

'I'll bring you a turmeric latte. And one of the pecan and apricot muffins from the bakery round the corner,' she said, knowing his weaknesses well.

'All right. As it's you. I've really got to go, sweetie. Let me know how you get on.'

'Yes, boss,' she said, even though he'd already hung up.

* * *

At twenty-five minutes past two, Mariana walked into the reception area of the gleaming glass and chrome building where Angelo Beresford worked, and asked for his secretary.

Two minutes later, a smartly dressed middle-aged woman approached her. 'Miss Thackeray?'

'Yes.'

'Mr Beresford will see you now.'

The paintings in the reception area were all modern abstracts, Mariana noticed, in keeping with the style of the ultra-modern glass and chrome building. It was a far cry from the kind of art she was studying. The painting must belong to a client, then, rather than to the firm of solicitors.

At half past two on the dot she was shown into Angelo Beresford's office.

Even though she'd looked him up on the website and discovered that he was a real hotshot in the firm and their youngest partner ever, in the flesh he wasn't quite what she'd expected. He had the kind of dark hair that would turn curly if he let it grow, dark eyes, a sensual mouth, and the longest eyelashes she'd ever seen.

He was absolutely gorgeous. And, when he smiled, her heart actually skipped a beat.

Not that she should let herself react like that. This was business. And, apart from anything else, she knew better than to trust to physical attraction. She'd made that mistake before, and it had ended really badly—to the point where she'd given up on relationships because she didn't trust her own judgement any more.

'Thank you for coming, Miss Thackeray.' He shook her hand, and a tingle went through her, despite her intentions to damp down that flare of attraction. 'May I offer you some coffee? Or something cold?'

'Thank you, but I'm fine.' She sat down on the chair he gestured to. 'How can I help?'

For a moment, Angelo's mouth went dry. He'd thought Mariana Thackeray was beautiful on the screen, but in real life he hadn't expected her to be quite as stunning. Surely the television make-up artists had exaggerated her features? But, although her glorious hair had been caught back at the nape of her neck and she wore no make-up whatsoever, she was still easily the most beautiful woman he'd seen in a long time—the more so because she didn't seem to realise it. And when she'd shaken his hand a second ago it had felt almost like an electric shock.

He needed to get a grip. This was business. He didn't do personal any more.

'I have a proposition for you, Miss Thackeray.' Oh, help. That sounded bad. He didn't mean it like that. Well, maybe his libido did, but he wasn't giving in to that pull of attraction. It couldn't go anywhere, even if it was reciprocated, so he'd smother it now. 'A job.'

She frowned. 'Your letter spoke about discussing a painting, not a job.'

'It's one and the same.' He sat down. 'My grandfather collected art. He'd like his collection to be in a gallery.'

'I can certainly recommend somewhere suitable, if he'd like to donate his collection,' she said.

'No, he wants to set up his own gallery,' Angelo said. 'But he needs the paintings to be catalogued and authenticated. One of them in particular.'

'Surely he was given the provenance when he bought the paintings?'

'Let's just say his paperwork's a bit on the slapdash side,' Angelo said. 'And some of the artwork is unsigned.'

'Which means you need someone to find a paper trail and do scientific investigations to prove that the works are what you think they are.'

He smiled, liking the way she'd picked up his train of thought so quickly. 'Exactly. Which is why you'd be perfect for the job. Plus my grandfather's seen your programme and he's taken a shine to you.'

'How much art are we talking about?' she asked.

'Framed, about forty or fifty pieces. Un-framed—' He shook his head. 'I'm afraid I have absolutely no idea. He collected for forty years.'

She looked at him as if she was assessing the scale of the project. As if she was really tempted. And then her blue eyes were filled with regret. 'Thank you for the opportunity, Mr Beresford,' she said, 'but I can't take on a project that big. Not with my studies and my work on *Hidden Treasure.*'

'Your studies are on the Macchiaioli—the Italian Impressionists,' he said. 'My grandfather has a lot of paintings by Lega, Fattori, Boldini and Carulli.' The artists she was studying. Would this be enough to tip the balance in his favour?

'So the painting in your letter…?'

'It's unsigned,' he said. 'But my grandfather believes that it's by Carulli.'

To his relief, her expression changed very slightly. So she *was* interested. Good.

'Do you have the painting here, Mr Beresford?'

Now for the tricky bit. 'No. It's at my grandfather's house in Florence.'

'Florence?' Her eyes widened in obvious surprise. 'I'm sorry, I can't just drop everything and go to Florence.'

'On what might turn out to be a wild goose chase? Quite. I wouldn't expect you to.' He took a cardboard wallet from the drawer and handed it to her. 'I took photographs of a few of the paintings at the weekend on my phone.

I'm afraid they're not professional quality because I took them all just where they hung in the house. I didn't want Nonno to ask what I was doing, in case you said no. But I did zoom in on the signatures as well, so I hope that will give you a better idea of exactly what he has.' And please, please, let it be enough for her to help him. To let him fulfil his grandfather's dreams before Leo Moretti died.

She opened the wallet and took out the photographs. She studied them closely, but there was no sign of recognition on her face. 'I don't know these works, but the styles are familiar,' she said.

Then she turned to the last photograph. The important one.

'This is the one you want me to investigate.' There was a slight crack in her voice, which told him the picture had definitely affected her. That was a good sign.

'That's the main one, yes, but I want you to check out all of them,' he said. 'Obviously I'll pay you a consultancy fee.' And he named a sum that was more than double what the media said she earned each year from the television programme. 'I'm happy to draw up a contract so everything is official.'

She stared at the photograph. 'I can't authenticate a painting from a photograph. I need to examine the actual painting, and I need to see a proper paper trail for the provenance—or as much of it as you have.'

'Then come to Florence and see the paintings for yourself,' he said.

She looked torn. So she was considering it; he just needed another sweetener to tip the balance. As Leo's executor, he had the power to make decisions.

'It wouldn't just be authenticating them,' he said. 'The family would give you exclusive access to the painting for your studies, before the gallery opens.' Which, if his grandfather was right and the paintings were genuine, could make a huge difference to her thesis.

'What do you know about that painting?' she asked.

'Just that he bought it in the nineteen-sixties, somewhere in England. The paperwork is probably in his files.' Honesty compelled him to add, 'But he hates filing. His paperwork is a total mess and I wouldn't even know where to start sorting it out.'

'I'm about to get really busy with the new series,' she said. 'Maybe if I start with the unsigned one and, if the initial investigations check out, we might be able to use it as part of the show—but I'd still need to get my producer's agreement for that. And then, after the summer, I could consider working on the rest.'

After the summer would be too late. 'I need you to work on them *now*, Miss Thackeray,' Angelo said, keeping his tone cool and calm but very definite.

'Why?'

The thing he'd been trying to make himself come to terms with for the last month. The thing that broke what was left of his heart into tiny, tiny shards. 'Because my grandfather is dying. He has lung cancer. He was in remission, but his last check-up at the hospital showed that it's back and they can't operate. All they can offer him now is palliative care.'

She looked horrified, and he realised he'd been too harsh. But there wasn't a nice way to say that someone you loved was dying. There just wasn't. The only way he could cope was to use cold, hard facts. 'Because I'm the lawyer in the family, he's asked me to be his executor. His will says he wants his collection authenticated and shown off in a gallery—but I want that unsigned painting examined now and the proof found that it really is what he thinks it is, so he can die happy, knowing he was right all along. I love my grandfather, Miss Thackeray, and I want to make him happy.' Give him something to distract him in his last few weeks, something else to focus on rather than the disease that was eating away at every breath.

'Until I've examined the paintings myself and inspected the backs,' she said, 'I can't promise anything. And I'd need to get my producer's agreement about using that unsigned painting on the show.'

'Why do you want to see the backs of the paintings?' he asked, not understanding.

'There are often markings and labels which can help trace its provenance. But I should warn you that there have been lots of scandals over the years in the art world. Copies, forgeries, and even forgeries of forgeries.'

'So you're saying my grandfather's paintings could be fakes.' Which meant that he was risking making his grandfather's final weeks miserable, taking all hope away. He didn't want to do that. But he didn't want his grandfather to die full of regrets, either.

'Or good reproductions, or maybe copies. If we can find paperwork for the provenance, that will help.' She looked at him. 'Why did you ask me to help?'

'Because my grandfather and my sister like your show,' he said. 'Nonno says you understand art. That you love it.'

'I do,' she agreed.

'And your biography on the *Hidden Treasure* website says that your studies are in the exact area of my grandfather's collection. Nineteenth-century Italian painters—the Macchiaioli, to be precise.'

Had he looked her up on only the *Hidden Treasure* website? Or had he seen the other stuff that would come up on an Internet search of her name?

As if the thought showed on her face, he said gently, 'And I saw your interview. Sorry, that's not meant to be unkind. Just that it was the next thing on the search results.'

'I know.' But it also meant that he knew everything that Eric had done. What a fool she'd been. 'And you still want me to look at the paintings?'

'Yes, I do.' He looked straight at her. 'Speaking out like that takes courage. I admire what you did. And I admire the way that you've moved on, done something good with your life.'

She wasn't quite there yet, but she was trying. 'I wanted to help other people in my situation. The interview seemed like the best way.'

'I'm sorry,' he said quietly, 'that you went through something so horrible.'

'It's past,' she said. 'And I've moved on.' That wasn't completely true. She'd completed her MA and started her PhD, forged a new career. She'd proved to herself that she wasn't the pathetic mess Eric had wanted her to believe she was. But she hadn't dated anyone since Eric. She couldn't trust herself not to get it so badly wrong as she had last time.

And this wasn't about relationships. Yes, so far, Angelo Beresford seemed like a nice guy. He'd been sensitive about her past. And he was attractive—he would've made a perfect artist's model. But for all she knew he could be in a committed relationship. Even if he wasn't, it didn't meant that anything could happen between them. She didn't trust herself—either to find the right person for her, or to make it work. This was going to be strictly business.

'All right. I'll come to Florence and see the paintings.'

'Good. Tomorrow?' he asked.

She stared at him. *'Tomorrow?'*

'I know it sounds like a rush.' Though he didn't sound in the slightest bit apologetic.

'It *is* a rush,' she corrected.

'Time's the one thing I don't have,' he said.

She thought of her own grandfather and how much she missed him since his death; she would have done anything to help him in his last days. Anything to make him smile instead of looking so lost and desolate, the light in his eyes gone. Clearly Angelo Beresford wanted to do the same for his grandfather. Who was she to deny that? 'All right,' she said.

'May I have your mobile number?' Angelo asked. 'I'll get my secretary to book the flight and contact you with the details.' He took a business card from his desk and scribbled something on the back. 'My private mobile, email and address, and my office details on the front,' he said, handing the card to her. 'If you do think the paintings are worth working on, what happens next?'

Now she was on safer ground. Work, not emotions. 'I'd photograph them, front and back,' she said. 'Then I'd set up a computer file for each one and work through the provenance.'

'How long would that take?'

'Photographing, maybe half an hour for each one. Less if I have someone to help me take them down from the walls and put them on an easel. The paperwork really depends—I can do some things online, but I'll also need to look at any paperwork your grandfather has. I'd like to talk to him about each of the paintings and for him to tell me what he remembers about them, if he's well enough.'

'Nonno's always well enough to talk about art,' Angelo said. He looked as if he was weighing up her words, working something out. 'So if we allow, say, three days to take the photographs, and a couple of days to talk about the paintings, we can fly back to London next Friday.'

She blinked. 'Are you serious? You want me to spend practically a week in Florence? With no notice?'

'I want the project done as soon as possible,' Angelo said. 'You can stay at the *palazzo* with us, or I can book a suite in a hotel for you if you'd prefer.'

Stay at a complete stranger's home—even if he was an elderly man in his final days? This was all going way too fast for her. 'I haven't even seen the paintings yet. Until I have, I can't make any promises.'

'My grandfather believes they're genuine, Miss Thackeray, and I trust his judgement. Give me that week. I'll book a hotel for you.

If you come to Florence with me tomorrow, see the paintings and you think I'm wasting your time, then that gives you a few days' holiday. If you don't think it's a waste of time, then that's a few days of work with some art that I'm guessing will be useful for your studies. Either way, I will pay you a consultancy fee for your time.'

Florence. Where, if the paintings turned out to be a disappointment, she could visit the Galleria d'Arte Moderna at the Pitti Palace, her favourite place in the city, and see some of the paintings she was studying. On the other hand, this could þe the chance to see some paintings by her favourite artists that had been lost for decades…

How could she turn down an opportunity like this? 'All right.' She took one of her own business cards from her handbag. 'That's my work mobile number.' She scribbled down some more information on the back. 'And my private mobile and email.'

'I'll let you know the flight times and I'll arrange for a taxi to take you to the airport in the morning,' he said. 'Thank you, Miss

Thackeray. If you give my secretary your bank details on your way out, I'll transfer a consultancy fee for your time.' He named a sum that made her eyes widen.

'Working on the basis that you're right about the collection, I'll need to bring my camera, tripod, photographic lights and an easel,' she said. 'Plus my laptop. And I'd prefer them to travel with me in the cabin rather than in the hold.'

'Noted. I'll organise the baggage details. And if you can give my secretary your passport details,' he said, 'she'll check you in on the flight.'

In some ways, this was surreal. But it was also the first time she'd felt properly enthusiastic about something since the court case. Maybe this would be the tipping point, the thing that finally helped her to move on and put the past completely behind her.

'I'll go home now and arrange it,' she said.

'Thank you, Miss Thackeray. I appreciate it.' He held out his hand to shake hers.

Again, her skin actually tingled where it met his. She'd have to be very careful not to let her attraction to him get in the way. She knew what she was doing where work was concerned, but relationships were a very different matter. Something she really wasn't good at.

'May I borrow those photographs?' she asked. 'So I can talk to my producer.'

'Of course.'

'Thank you.'

On the way home, Mariana used her phone to snap the photographs, emailed the images to Nigel, and then called him.

'I'm just out of the meeting and I've emailed you some photographs. Here's the elevator pitch. Imagine the equivalent of a chateau full of lost paintings by Degas, Monet and Pisarro. And the owner wants me to catalogue them all and check out the provenance of some of them.'

'No way,' Nigel said. 'No *way* is there a chateau full of lost French Impressionists.'

'*Equivalent*,' she reminded him. 'It's a *palazzo* in Florence, so we're talking Italian rather than French Impressionists. It's the Macchiaioli, the ones I'm studying. And I'm going to see the paintings tomorrow.'

'What?'

'Angelo Beresford wants me to authenticate the paintings—and the painting in that last shot I sent you is unsigned. If it's what my gut tells me it is, then it'd be perfect for the show.'

'If something sounds too good to be true, Mariana, it usually is.'

Yeah. She knew that one first-hand from the lovely, sweet, gentle man she thought she'd got engaged to—the man who'd turned out to be a control freak with a nasty temper behind the charm. The man who'd almost broken her. 'It's worth a look,' she said. 'Just think, Nigel. *A whole collection*. Art that hasn't been seen for decades.' Even the idea made her heart rate go up a few notches.

'So, on the basis of a few photographs, you're planning to go to Florence tomorrow with a stranger.'

'A lawyer in a very respectable firm that has very posh offices in the city, and he checks out as genuine,' she corrected.

'But the man's still a stranger.'

'We're working on the third series of the

show now. How many lost paintings have we found so far?' she asked.

'Fourteen, and two where we couldn't prove the provenance or get them accepted by the experts, but the detective side of the story made really good viewing,' Nigel said. 'Along with all the hundreds of people who've contacted us about fakes and copies.'

'I think it's worth following up,' she said. 'I haven't had a holiday in a year and a half. Worst-case scenario, if it *is* too good to be true, then I'll get a few days' break in Florence. Best-case, if this is an eccentric collector and the paintings are genuine, they'll fit in with my PhD and make a potential episode of *Hidden Treasure*—and I think it'll be our best episode to date.'

'You really want to do this, don't you?'

She nodded. 'I've got a funny feeling about it.'

'More like you really want it to be true,' Nigel said. 'Like if someone told me they had what they thought was a lost Turner painting and we looked into it for *Hidden Treasure* and managed to find the provenance. I'd be thrilled.'

'Exactly.'

Nigel sighed. 'I'd be happier if someone went with you.'

Mariana knew what he was worrying about. 'Eric isn't going to come after me,' she said. 'There's a restraining order in place.'

'Which he broke last year.'

'And he has a suspended sentence. He's not going to risk spending at least two years in prison,' Mariana said. 'So I'm going to Florence. I'll keep you posted.'

She was lucky, Mariana thought as she walked from the tube station to her flat. So very lucky.

Lucky that she had a family and friends who'd refused to give up on her when Eric had started to isolate her from everyone. Lucky that they'd seen through his charm when she hadn't been able to—and then that they'd seen her failing self-esteem and bolstered her. Lucky that they'd got her into a refuge when things turned nasty and then helped her get a restraining order so he couldn't come anywhere near her again.

Eric had lied in court. He'd said that she was

making it all up. That she was a drama queen begging for attention and she might as well have been on one of those 'court case' reality TV shows rather than in a proper court of law.

But the court had seen the truth. That he'd systematically undermined her over the two years of their relationship, made her feel useless and worthless, and isolated her from her family and friends. And her lawyer had found one of his exes; Eric had treated Adele in exactly the same way, and she'd been willing to speak up in court.

The court had made the injunction with no reservations.

And how Eric must hate it that she'd gone on to be happy. That she'd finished her MA in History of Art and then landed the job presenting *Hidden Treasure*. That she was well on the way to becoming Dr Mariana Thackeray and people respected her for her knowledge.

He'd tried to bring her down when *Hidden Treasure* first started airing. He'd posted anonymous comments on social media, hinting that she was unstable and untrustworthy. In the end, to squash the rumours and to make sure the truth was told properly, she'd told her story to the national press and made sure that the fee went to the women's refuge that had helped her. She really, really hoped that she'd helped other people in that situation and given them the courage to find an escape.

She'd come through the other side.

But she was never, ever going to get sucked into another relationship again. She'd learned that work and friendship were reliable; love and her judgement in men definitely weren't.

'We're flying to Florence tomorrow, Mamma,' Angelo said.

'And do you think she will do the job?' Lucrezia asked.

'I hope so. She needs to see the paintings for herself before she'll commit—which is fair.'

'Maybe I should come back from Rome.'

Where she was staying with his sister and the new baby.

Baby, Angelo thought, and shoved the thought aside before it started trampling on a sore spot. 'Don't cut your visit short, Mamma,' he said. He loved his mother dearly, but she had overdramatic tendencies—he rather thought she enjoyed playing up to the stereotypes of being Italian and being an opera singer—and the last thing he wanted was for his mother to scare Mariana off. 'It's fine. Nonno will have me to translate if he gets tired, and he has Lucia to look after him.' The housekeeper, who kept everything on an even keel and kept an eye on Leo for Angelo.

'Angelo. It breaks my heart seeing him fade and knowing I can do nothing to help.' Her voice cracked. 'Palliative care. *O mio babbino caro.*'

She was so upset that she was whispering the words rather than singing them as she usually would. Angelo dug his nails into his palms. He couldn't fix this. Nobody could. But he was going to make sure his grandfather was happy before they lost him for ever. He was going to bring joy to Leo Moretti's last days, whatever it took. 'I know, Mamma. It's hard.'

'And you're a good boy. So like your father. Roderick would be so proud of you.'

Angelo had followed in his father's footsteps as far as his career was concerned, even joining the same legal firm. His marriage and the children he'd thought he'd have were a very different matter.

'Would you have time to come and see us when you're in Italy?'

He knew what his mother wasn't saying. They all understood why he would find seeing the baby difficult. And he also knew he had to face it, for his sister's sake. He had to put his family's needs first instead of being self-ish and trying to protect himself from having old scars ripped open. 'If Mariana stays to do the photographs, I'll come up to Rome for the afternoon. I'll get the train.'

'Try, Angelo. Cammie worries.'

His younger sister was far less dramatic, but he took the point. 'I know, Mamma. And there is no need to worry. Everything is going to be just fine.'

He'd make sure it was.

CHAPTER TWO

'MUM, YOU DON'T have to drop everything and come to Florence with me,' Mariana protested. 'I'll be fine.'

'You don't know this man. He could be anyone,' Carol Thackeray said, her mouth thinning. 'And does your injunction even apply abroad?'

'Mum.' Mariana took both her mother's hands. 'I love you. And I'm not doing anything risky, I promise. The guy's a partner in a really big firm of lawyers in the city—I met him at his office this afternoon and it's all legit. He clearly loves his grandfather, who's dying. Angelo is dropping everything to make him happy before the end, and I can understand that. I'm sure you can, too.'

'Oh, darling. I know you miss your grandfather. I miss him, too. And, yes, of course I can understand. But this worries me.' Carol frowned. 'I can come with you.'

'Mum, your idea of hell is being stuck indoors or being dragged round a dusty art gallery when there's a garden outside with roses to be pruned and borders to weed,' Mariana said with a smile. 'You don't have to do that. And I want to go. If I spend the rest of my life looking over my shoulder and worrying, that means Eric wins. I want to live my life as I want to, Mum. Independently. *Well*. The way I promised Grandad I would.'

Carol sighed. 'Then I want you to text me. A lot.'

'I will. And I'll send photographs,' Mariana promised.

'Hey, Cammie. How are you and my gorgeous niece doing?' Angelo asked his sister.

'Fine.'

He coughed. 'This is a video call, Cammie. I can see your face.'

His sister looked around, and whispered, 'Mamma's fussing is driving me insane!'

'She's just worried about you.'

'Remember when she had that two weeks in London playing *Lucia di Lammermoor* in Covent Garden and stayed with you? Imagine that, times a thousand.'

Angelo couldn't suppress a grin.

'It's not funny, Angelo. Just you wait until you have—' She stopped, her face stricken.

Yeah. He knew what she'd almost said. *Until you have a baby and Mamma decides she has to stay with you for a month to 'help out'.* Except he couldn't actually have children. Which was why Stephanie had dumped him; and he'd been wary about starting another relationship since. What was the point, when he couldn't give a woman what she really wanted—when he'd totally failed at being a husband? Much better to avoid the risk of rejection and not let anyone else into his life.

'I'm sorry, Angelo. I didn't mean—'

'I know you didn't, Cammie. It's OK,' he cut in. 'Really. I was just calling to see how you all are. And I hope to come up to see you next week. It's about time I met my niece. Serafina's two weeks old already.'

'I'll understand if you don't w—'

'Of course I want to come and see her, Cammie. She's yours and Ed's. I can't wait to meet her.' And he meant it. He'd ignore the fact that his heart ached for what might have been. For the babies he'd never have.

'You can really get the time off work to come and see us?'

'I'm delegating a lot and I'm working out of the office as much as I can,' Angelo said. 'I want to spend time with Nonno.' While he was still here.

'I'd love to bring the baby to see him,' Camilla said, 'except I worry it might be too much for him.'

'And for you and Serafina,' Angelo said, mindful that Serafina had been a month premature. 'You must be worn out with night feeds and nappy changes.'

'I'm a bit sleep-deprived,' his sister admitted. 'But I'll manage. Mamma says that Mariana Thackeray has agreed to look at Nonno's paintings.'

'I'm bringing her to Florence tomorrow. And hopefully seeing the paintings at the *palazzo* will convince her to take the job,' Angelo said.

'And then keep your fingers crossed that we can find everything out we need for Nonno. Get that painting authenticated.' In the few weeks they had left before their grandfather died.

'Even if it doesn't work out,' Camilla said gently, 'you've done your best, and he'll know that. It's enough, Angelo.'

No, it wasn't. But he wasn't going to make her miserable by arguing.

'Let me know when you're coming. I can't wait to see you.'

'I will. Lots of love to you all,' Angelo said, and tried to ignore the guilt he felt at not supporting his sister better.

It was just... *Babies.*

To distract himself, he moved a couple of books on the shelves; and then he wished he hadn't when a small cardboard wallet fell onto the floor.

He knew exactly what was in it.

He knew he shouldn't look.

And yet he couldn't help opening the wallet and taking them out. Photographs that an old family friend had taken on their wedding day and sent copies.

How young they looked. How happy. Literally glowing with joy, Stephanie's golden hair bright in the sunlight.

And how easily it had all faded. How quickly love—or what he had thought was love—had vanished, submerged beneath Stephanie's need for a baby. Lovemaking had turned from a spontaneous joy to a clinical planning of having sex at the most fertile times in her cycle.

When two years of trying to have a baby had ended in failure, they'd gone for tests. They'd both been shocked to discover that, thanks to a bout of mumps nobody really remembered him having as a young child, Angelo was practically infertile. The only way they'd have a baby of their own was with the help of gruelling IVF treatment which had no guarantee of success; the odds were one in four.

Stephanie hadn't been able to face that.

But she also hadn't wanted to try fostering or adoption. She wanted the whole deal—pregnancy and a baby, but without any complications.

After a month of fighting, she'd walked out and divorced him on the grounds of irreconcilable differences. Financially, she'd been fair rather than taking him to the cleaners. But Angelo would've given anything—*everything*—to have been able to make things all right again. To have given his wife what she wanted with no complications. To have been *enough* for her.

Though there was no point in whining for what you couldn't have.

Since the divorce, he'd concentrated on work. And he knew he'd withdrawn a little from his family. Kept his emotions under lock and key. It had taken Camilla three months to find the words to tell him that he was going to be an uncle. And she'd cried when she told him—not tears of joy for her unborn child, but tears for the pain she thought she'd caused him. He'd hated himself for ruining what should've been a moment of sheer joy.

He dragged in a breath. *Not now.* This wasn't about the mess of his past. And he wasn't in love with Stephanie any more. He was at the stage where he could wish his ex-wife happiness—where he could actually be pleased that she'd got what she wanted. A new partner, a new baby.

And he was genuinely pleased for his sister, even though his heart ached for what he wasn't able to have himself.

But he wasn't prepared to risk losing his heart to anyone again. To risk being rejected again.

On Saturday morning, he sent Mariana Thackeray a text from the airport.

Am by the check-in desk.

His phone pinged with an immediate response.

In taxi. About fifteen minutes away.

He busied himself answering emails, and when he looked up Mariana was walking across to him.

'Thank you for coming, Miss Thackeray,' he said. 'My grandfather's looking forward to meeting you.'

'I'm looking forward to meeting him,' she

said politely. 'And I think, in the circumstances, maybe we should use first names. I'm Mariana.'

'Angelo,' he responded.

And he was going to ignore the fact that her smile made his heart feel a bit lighter. This wasn't about him. This was about fixing things for his grandfather.

Once they'd checked in, he bought them coffee and pastries, and they made small talk until their flight was called.

Once they were on the plane, he thought maybe this was a chance to understand her better, work out what made her tick. 'So how did you get into art history?' he asked.

'I always liked paintings, even when I was tiny. My grandfather used to take me to all the galleries—he loved art and museums,' she said. 'My mother always says that Tate Britain, the National and the Courtauld are my second homes.' She smiled again. 'I guess I do spend a lot of time there.'

'You never thought about being an artist yourself?'

She laughed. 'Sadly, I can barely draw a

straight line with a ruler, so art school was never an option. But I love history, so a degree in history of art seemed the way to go. I planned to be a curator.'

'And you did your MA part-time.'

'Yes.' She paused. 'I worked part-time in a gallery, too.'

She looked slightly awkward, and he guessed that it was something to do with her ex. Had he made her feel that she'd never make it in her chosen career? Not that Angelo would be unkind enough to ask.

'How did you get to present *Hidden Treasure*?' he asked instead.

'One of my tutors—the one who supervises my PhD now—knew Nigel and suggested me for an interview and screen test. I'd never worked in television before, but Nigel was prepared to take a risk. Luckily my interview was all about tracing provenance, so it was something where I had experience and I could talk about. Nigel gave me a chance, and now we're making the third series. I'm just so lucky to be able to do something I love so much for a living.'

He could tell she really was grateful, not paying lip service or taking it for granted; and her joy in her job shone in her eyes.

'There's a lot to be said for that.' He loved his job, too. And he was so grateful he'd been able to bury himself in work when his marriage collapsed.

'What about you?' she asked.

Was she being polite, or was she really interested? 'I followed in my father's footsteps,' he said. 'Dad died from a heart attack ten years ago, so I didn't get to work with him like I'd planned to, but his old firm offered me a job in their Mergers and Acquisitions team when I qualified, and I worked my way up.'

'You never wanted to be an art collector or an artist?'

'Like my grandfather, you mean? No. I loved staying in Florence with him and my grandmother every summer, and I've probably seen every piece of art in the city with the pair of them, but Nonno always says that Cammie— my sister, who's an accountant—and Mamma are the only ones who appreciate art.'

'Your mother's a painter or collector?'

'No.' He looked at her. 'Are you interested in any of the other arts, Mariana?'

'Yes.'

'Then you might have heard of her. Lucrezia Moretti—she kept her maiden name professionally.'

'I'm sorry,' she said. 'I'm afraid her name isn't familiar.'

He smiled. 'I grew up with it, but I know opera isn't to everyone's taste.'

She blinked. 'Your mother's an opera singer?'

He inclined his head. 'She's officially retired now. But every so often she can be tempted back on stage by a director she admires, if the role is right. Though the artistic genes have bypassed me.'

'You don't have to be able to make art to appreciate it,' she said.

'Sometimes it's hard to appreciate it. I understand why my grandfather thinks I'm a philistine—I hated being dragged round an art gallery or a museum as a child when I could've been outside running around a garden instead,' he said. 'To be honest, I still feel a bit that way. I'd rather walk by the river or in a garden.'

She smiled. 'My mother's the same. Garden centres for her are like art galleries for me. She says she'd rather be able to smell the flowers than look at a painting of them.'

'Your mother,' he said, 'sounds wise.'

'So what made you pick law as a career?' she asked.

'Listening to my dad talk about fairness and making things right. I admired him, and I wanted to do the same kind of thing that he did. My mother is very dramatic and—' he grimaced '—it feels mean saying this, but she was a bit chaotic, when I was a child. Being an opera singer, she's meant to be flamboyant, but sometimes I found it a bit too much to handle. I liked things calm and organised. I was happiest when Dad and I took the dog for a walk by the river at the crack of dawn and everything was quiet—kind of an oasis.' He smiled. 'Sad to say, I was probably the only teenage boy in the history of the world who never got yelled at to tidy his room, because it was always neat and tidy.'

She looked slightly worried, and he remembered what he'd read about her ex in that article. 'I'm a neat freak, and I'm probably a bit of a control freak where my work's concerned, but I do try to listen to my colleagues and be fair. So please tell me if I say or do anything that makes you uncomfortable, because I don't want you to feel worried about anything.'

'Thank you. I appreciate that.'

Maybe she'd open up more if he asked her about the task in hand. 'How exactly do you evaluate a painting? What evidence do you look for?'

'I'm assuming you want the general outline first, rather than my plan for any one specific painting?' she asked.

'The specifics can come later. A generalisation would give me a useful background.' Angelo pushed away the thought that he really liked seeing the animation in Mariana's face when she talked about art, the passion in her blue eyes. This wasn't about her or that flare of attraction that he needed to ignore; it was about making his grandfather's dream come true.

'I'd start by measuring the painting, then

I'd record the dimensions, a description of the frame, the medium—oils, watercolour, pastels or whatever—whether it's signed, the style and the subject, and if there's any inscription or anything on the frame. Then I'd check the back of the painting for exhibition marks, dealer stamps, gallery labels and any signs of previous ownership.'

She'd mentioned that before, and he hadn't quite understood why. 'The back of the painting's that important?'

'Yes. There's a lot of information you can add to catalogue notes.' She took her laptop out of her bag and flicked into the photo app. 'Here's an example of the kind of thing I mean.' She showed him a photograph of the back of the painting. 'There's a label on the back here,' she said, pointing to it, 'which tells us that this painting was in an exhibition. I can check that, and find contemporary reviews. I'd add those into the catalogue notes as well. There's another label there—' she pointed to it '—from the dealer, so I can look at the dealer's records to confirm when, where and from whom the dealer bought it. And here, this stamp tells us who manufactured the canvas, so we can narrow the dates of the painting down to when that manufacturer was active.'

'I had no idea you could tell so much from the back,' Angelo said.

'You can tell other things, too. A light-coloured canvas could indicate a more modern date than the painting's meant to be, hinting that it's a copy. An extra lining might mean restoration work. If you took the frame off completely, you should see that there isn't a straight edge to the paint on the canvas—if there is, it might be a reproduction or cut down.'

He stored that all away for future reference. 'So that's all the physical stuff you need?'

'No. The front's important, too. You can use comparative techniques to look at the colours the artist uses and the brush work, plus the composition. There should be similarities to other works by the artist. There may be sketches and studies to help date it. We can evaluate the pigments to make sure they match the age of the painting. X-rays can show if the painting has been altered, and if there are any sketches underneath; and sometimes painters reused canvases, so again that can help to give evidence that the artist has a connection to the piece.'

'That makes sense,' Angelo said. And he really liked the way she seemed so systematic and professional rather than vague. She definitely knew what she was talking about, and she put things into layman's terms without being pompous or patronising. No wonder the producer had snapped her up as a presenter.

'Then, once you've looked at all the physical evidence and your list of things to check, you gather the paper evidence for provenance—which basically traces the movements of a painting from the moment it leaves an artist's studio to where it is now,' she explained. 'Establishing who owned it, when it was sold and how much for, will help to authenticate the painting.'

Angelo blinked. 'So how do you actually prove all that?'

'In your grandfather's case, you can start with when he bought each painting, where and who from, and trace that back through who owned it before him, and the idea is to get back as far as you can,' Mariana said. 'If he bought it from a dealer, then the dealer would probably have a lot of that information already. You can check catalogues and exhibition listings, too. If the trail breaks, you start at the other end, from the painter's studio.'

'That could take a really long time.' Time they didn't have.

Either he'd spoken his thoughts aloud or his dismay showed on his face, because she said gently, 'If we start with that unsigned picture, that's the important one. And I can access extra help to look up sources if it's part of *Hidden Treasure.*'

He'd just have to hope there was enough evidence to convince her. That she'd fall in love with the painting. And that his grandfather would hold on for long enough for them to get the results.

Once they'd landed at Pisa, Mariana texted her mother to let her know she'd arrived and they took the train to Florence, enjoying the views of the Tuscan countryside and the River Arno along the way. The sky was a brilliant blue and the sun was warm. It was a perfect day, she thought. And she was surprised by how much she enjoyed Angelo's company. He was easy to be with, actually listened to her, and asked sensible questions. Though it was more than that. Something she couldn't quite put her finger on—or maybe didn't quite dare face.

'Should we get a taxi to your hotel?' Angelo asked when they'd disembarked.

'If it's in the centre, I'd rather walk,' Mariana said. 'By the time we've found a taxi and negotiated our way through the city, we could've walked there.'

'Then we'll walk. Provided you let me carry at least half your bags, because you have much more luggage than I do.'

'That's kind. Thank you.' She let him take charge of the easel and the lights.

Once she'd checked into the hotel and sent her mother a text to confirm her safe arrival, she followed Angelo through the city.

'I love Florence,' she said wistfully. 'On every corner there seems to be a church or a gorgeous building; but it's the little details I always notice. Look at those tiny bronze tortoises holding up grilles on that window.' She gestured towards them. 'And that enormous lion's head over there on that door knocker. And the Medici symbol on a stone shield on the corner of that *palazzo*.'

'Either I really am a philistine, or familiarity breeds contempt,' Angelo said, 'because I never really notice things like that.'

'Did you come to Florence often when you were younger?' she asked.

'Cammie and I stayed with our grandparents here every summer,' he said. 'Though I probably didn't appreciate the city as much as I should've done. It's beautiful. But I guess I see the wood, and you're seeing the individual trees as well.'

Brunelleschi's red-tiled dome loomed up against the sky; and then finally the cathedral itself came into view, the beautiful pink and green and white facade with its rose windows and niches filled with statues, next to the tall square bell tower and the huge octagonal baptistery.

'I love this city. It's probably my favourite after London,' she said. 'The way that anywhere you walk, you see something beautiful, whether it's the reproduction of David next to the entrance of the Palazzo Vecchio, or the narrow streets that suddenly open into wide squares.'

Funny, walking with her made him see the city with new eyes. And somehow she made the old, familiar place feel fresh and full of wonder.

Finally Angelo stopped by a large dark brown building. 'Welcome to the Palazzo dei Gigli,' he said.

'The Palace of Lilies?' she translated.

'Yes. And here are the lilies.' He pointed to the tiny fleurs-de-lys decorating the windows and lintels, a mixture of carved stone and wrought iron.

'They're gorgeous. Can I take a photo?' She gestured to her phone.

He smiled. 'Of course. Nonno will be pleased you like the lilies. They're from the sixteenth century, I think.'

'They're beautiful,' she said. 'Excuse me a second.' She quickly texted her mother to say she had arrived at the *palazzo*.

Angelo opened the door, then stood aside for her.

'Nonno?' he called when he'd closed the front door behind them.

'Angelo!' A woman bustled over to him, hugged him and kissed him on each cheek. She said something in rapid Italian that Mariana couldn't quite catch.

'Let me introduce you,' Angelo said. 'Lucia, this is Mariana Thackeray, who's come to look at Nonno's paintings. Mariana, this is Lucia, who looks after Nonno and takes a lot of worry off my shoulders.'

'Pleased to meet you, Mariana,' Lucia said in a strong accent.

'And you, Lucia,' Mariana said politely.

'Is Nonno asleep?' Angelo asked.

'No. He's in the Red Room,' Lucia said. 'I'll make coffee.'

'No need, Lucia, thank you,' Angelo said. 'It's practically lunchtime and I was planning to take Nonno out.'

'*Bene*. You tell me if you need anything,' she said, and kissed his cheeks again. 'You are a good boy to your *nonno*. Your *mamma* brought you up well.' She patted his arm and left.

Mariana glanced round the hallway. The walls were crammed with paintings of various sizes, and she recognised some of them from the photographs Angelo had shown her.

'This is amazing,' she whispered.

'Don't look too closely,' he said. 'I think Nonno is looking forward to showing them to you himself and he'll enjoy seeing the reaction of a fellow art-lover.' He set his case down in the space under the stairs and shepherded Mariana into a living room.

'Nonno, we have a guest,' he said. 'Mariana Thackeray is here to meet you.'

An elderly man, his face sallow and his cheeks thin, sat in one of the winged armchairs; although the day was warm, he had a blanket over his knees.

'Please, don't get up,' Mariana said, and hurried over to him. *'Piacere di conoscerla*, Signor Moretti.'

'Buongiorno, Signorina Thackeray,' he said. 'I have looked forward to meeting you. I love

your television show.' He coughed. '*Mi dispiace*. Lucia is getting coffee, yes?'

'No, because I am taking you out to lunch, Nonno.' Angelo hugged the old man warmly and spoke in rapid Italian.

'Manners, Angelo. We speak English with our guest,' Leo admonished. 'I may call you Mariana?' he asked, turning to her.

'Of course,' she said.

'And I am Leo. Thank you for coming all this way to see my paintings.'

'It's my pleasure.'

'Your show has just started here in Italy,' he said. 'And you find out the truth about the paintings.'

'I do,' she said. 'Though I should warn you it's not always good news. We have had some that haven't been accepted by the experts.'

'But if anyone can prove my painting...' He coughed again.

He had lung cancer, Mariana remembered. 'Can I get anything for you?' she asked. 'A glass of water or something?'

'No, no, child. Thank you. But I would like to show you my *Girl*.'

The unsigned painting, she guessed. The one he hoped was a Carulli.

'Come with me,' he said.

'Nonno, let me help,' Angelo said, supporting his grandfather as Leo got to his feet.

Angelo Beresford might be a little bit on the bossy side and run everything to his personal timescale, Mariana thought, but he was patient and kind with his grandfather, and that spoke volumes about his character.

Leo beckoned to her to follow him. 'I have collected art for many years,' he said. 'And this is the first painting I bought, fifty years ago.' He stopped in front of a landscape.

Mariana looked and looked again, and all the hairs stood up on her arms. 'I've seen the preliminary sketches for this,' she said. 'Carulli. Everyone thought the painting itself was lost. I'm a bit shocked to actually see it.'

'I spent my youth travelling in Carulli's footsteps, and I bought every painting and every sketch I could find,' Leo said.

Mariana walked slowly along the hallway, drinking in the paintings. 'This is...' She shook her head, words failing her. 'Amazing,' she finished softly.

'Come and see my *Girl*, Mariana. The valuers say we can only say it is attributed to him, but I know it is *by* him.'

Mariana stared at the painting above the fireplace, and her jaw dropped. 'Oh, my God,' she whispered. 'It's…' Tears rose in her eyes at the sheer beauty of the large canvas in front of her. 'The photograph Angelo showed me doesn't begin to do it justice.'

'See. I told you she understands art,' Leo said to Angelo.

'That's why I asked her to come here,' Angelo said with a smile.

'It's the most beautiful painting I've ever seen in my life,' Mariana said.

It was very simple: a farmhouse in front of a field of corn that was scattered with poppies, and a woman with long dark hair and wearing a white dress was leaning out of the window.

'The Girl in the Window,' Leo said. 'Look at the light. The sky. The sunlight on the corn.'

'Her eyes. Her face.' She blinked back the tears. 'Sorry. It's just…'

'Don't apologise. She made me cry when I first saw her,' Leo said.

'Do you have the paperwork to go with this?'

'Some,' Leo said.

'Not enough to make the experts happy,' Angelo added.

'There is no signature. Do you know why?'

'Yes.' Leo looked at Angelo. 'Can you…?'

'Translate? Sure.' He listened while Leo spoke in Italian. 'The painting was stored in the attic of the house where it was painted,' Angelo translated. 'There was damage by mice. Nonno had it restored professionally, but the signature was eaten away.'

'It looks like Carulli's brushwork,' Mariana said, inspecting it closely. She took out a jeweller's loupe just to check, and to her relief the colour didn't resolve into a dot-matrix pattern. This wasn't simply a good reproduction: it was a real painting. 'My gut feel is that you're right and it *is* his, but my gut feel alone isn't enough to authenticate it. I need to study the painting properly and I might need to take it for tests— for X-rays and microscopic analysis. And I definitely need to take a look at the back and see any paper evidence you have, Leo.'

'So you're going to use it for the programme?' Angelo asked.

'I will lobby Nigel very, very hard,' she said. 'This is an incredible painting, and I think it might have an incredible story to go with it.'

Before she could say anything else, her phone rang.

'Please excuse me—I really do need to take this,' she said and answered it. 'Yes, Mum, I'm fine. The paintings are amazing and I'll ring you straight back on video call so you can see for yourself. Hang on.' She ended the call, then rang her mother back. 'Mum—I'd like to introduce you to two people.' She switched the camera orientation on her phone so her mother could see Leo and Angelo. 'Signor Moretti and Angelo, I would like to introduce you to my mother, Carol Thackeray.'

'*Buongiorno*, Signora Thackeray. I am Leo Moretti. This is my *palazzo* and these are my paintings,' Leo said.

'Hello, Mrs Thackeray. I'm Angelo Beresford, Leo's grandson and legal representative,' Angelo said.

'Hello to you both,' Carol said.

'And this is *the* painting, Mum,' Mariana said, turning the camera to the painting.

'Oh, my. It's lovely,' Carol said.

'Isn't it just? We're talking about it now. I'll call you later, Mum.' She ended the call. 'I'm sorry,' she said to Angelo and Leo. 'My mother worries about me travelling alone.'

'Mothers usually have good instincts,' Leo said.

Though her mother, too, had been taken in by Eric at first.

'So where do we go from here?' Angelo asked.

'I need to put as much evidence as I can together to convince Nigel,' she said. 'So if we could perhaps sit down together, Leo, and you tell me everything you can and let me see the paperwork, plus I will take more detailed photographs of the front and the back of the painting to get the physical evidence.'

'Ah. Paperwork.' Leo coughed. *'Mi scusi.'*

'Will you allow me to show Mariana your study, Nonno?' Angelo asked.

Leo sighed, and said something in Italian that Mariana couldn't translate.

Angelo supported his grandfather back to the Red Room, and made sure the blanket covered his knees.

'I warn you now, this isn't pretty,' Angelo said as he took Mariana to Leo's office. He opened the door and she could see boxes piled haphazardly everywhere. 'It's what my sister calls the shoebox style of filing your receipts,' he said. 'And the boxes aren't even in order within themselves. If Nonno moved a box to get to a shelf, he didn't necessarily put it back, and then things have been put in that box out of order. Mamma, my sister Cammie and I have all offered to help him sort it out, but he won't let anyone touch it.' He rolled his eyes. 'I love my grandfather dearly, but I don't know how he can live with all this chaos. It would drive me crackers.'

She could see the genuine warmth in his eyes, mingled with frustration that he was clearly trying to suppress, and she felt for him.

Rather than bossing his grandfather around, he was trying to understand. Angelo Beresford was a good man.

'I'm assuming this is something you'd prefer the cameras not to see—though the camera crew will want to visit the *palazzo* to show the paintings in place, plus take shots of any documentary evidence you have,' Mariana said.

Angelo grimaced. 'I know you could explain it as all part of Nonno being an eccentric art collector, but I don't want people mocking my grandfather or saying he's like one of those hoarders whose house is a health hazard.'

'Of course you don't. And my programme isn't about that sort of thing. It's about appreciating art and sharing people's dreams.' She looked at him. 'Does your grandfather know where anything is among his, um, storage system?'

Angelo wrinkled his nose. 'We can ask, but I have a nasty feeling that he probably doesn't.'

'There's no way we'll find the evidence in here before Friday,' she said. 'I can sort through that paperwork and catalogue all the paintings for you, but it's going to take a lot of time and

I really can't do it in Florence. I need to be in London because I have weekly meetings with my supervisor about my thesis, and obviously we're working on the new series of *Hidden Treasure* so I'll have things to do for the show.'

'So where do you suggest we go from here?' he asked.

She liked the fact he was asking her advice rather than taking charge and making assumptions that might not be correct. This was a man who paid attention to detail—but who also thought beyond his own ego, and she appreciated that. 'I think the most sensible thing would be for me to photograph all the canvases here, framed and unframed, and then bring back the unframed sketches and all the paperwork to London.'

'We could bring everything back to my house,' Angelo said. 'That is, if you don't mind working there.'

'OK. I could do that.'

Just as they were about to go in search of Leo, Angelo's phone rang. He glanced at the screen. 'Excuse me. Would you mind if I answer that?'

'Please do,' she said.

He spoke in Italian so rapidly that she couldn't quite catch the gist of it. 'That was my mother,' he said when he ended the conversation. 'She worries about Nonno.'

'It's good to have family who care,' she said. If hers hadn't been close and looked out for her, Eric would have ground her down completely.

'Mamma's a bit torn at the moment. My sister Camilla had a baby two weeks ago, but Serafina was a month early and Mamma wants to be there to support Cammie—except Cammie lives in Rome, and meanwhile Nonno's getting frailer and Mamma wants to support him at the same time. I come back to Florence every weekend at the moment, but I have work commitments and I can't be here as much as I'd like to.' He took a deep breath and pain filled his eyes. 'We're all hoping that you visiting will make him a bit brighter.'

She remembered how that felt. She would've done anything to brighten her grandfather's days at the end. 'With the hope of authenticating his *Girl*, you mean?'

'Yes.'

She nodded. 'Though I don't want to tire him out.'

'What do you need from him?'

'As much information as he can give me. To save him having to walk round the *palazzo* with me, maybe I could take a photograph of each painting on my laptop and use them as a prompt. Then at least he can sit down while we talk and not have to stand.'

'Thank you for thinking about him. How good is your Italian?'

'I can get by,' she said, 'but if he talks too fast I won't be able to follow.'

'If I translate for you both, then you can ask what you want to know in English, and Nonno can answer in Italian.'

Mindful of how much Angelo was paying her in consultancy fees, Mariana said, 'Can we start today?'

'We should have lunch first.'

'All right. And we'll take everything at your grandfather's pace. He can rest when he needs to, and I can do other work in between.'

'Do you want me to fetch your equipment

from your hotel?' he asked. 'Or maybe we can kill two birds with one stone and have lunch there—we can pick up your equipment at the same time.'

'That,' she said, 'is a very good idea.'

CHAPTER THREE

THEY TOOK A taxi to Mariana's hotel; although it was within walking distance, clearly Angelo was worried about his grandfather getting overtired.

Once they'd ordered lunch, she said, 'Leo, please forgive me for asking, but do you know exactly what's in your paperwork?'

He spread his hands. 'What can I say? I never liked filing. Just as well I never actually had to work at the bank.'

'Bank?' she asked.

'Yes. My great-grandfather had a bank. All the men in my family worked there, until me. My father expected me to do it, too, but I knew I wasn't suited. I liked art.'

'Nothing wrong with that,' Mariana said.

Angelo smiled. 'And isn't there a tradition in Florence of bankers collecting art? The city is rich beyond measure, thanks to the Medici collectors.'

'Yes,' Leo said. 'When my father died, I sold the bank.' He looked at Angelo. 'What you said about the Medici—I want our family name remembered for our art collection, too.'

'Angelo told me you went to art school,' Mariana said. 'Did you think of becoming a painter rather than a collector?'

Leo shook his head. 'I was a competent draughtsman, but I knew I would never be more than that. But I have a good eye. I bought sketches and watercolours in flea markets and at fairs.'

'Did you keep the receipts?' she asked.

'I am the son of a banker. I know better than to throw away a receipt,' he said.

It was exactly what she'd hoped to hear. And there was one more thing that would really help. 'Did you ever keep a journal about your collecting?' she asked.

'*Sì*. Every year I had a new diary.' He smiled. 'Always the colour of good Tuscan wine.'

She went very still. Diaries. These could be really important. 'Are they all in your office?'

'Somewhere, in the boxes, yes,' he said.

She exchanged a glance with Angelo. If Leo had said in the diary exactly where and when he'd bought something, and maybe added in the details, it could really help with the paper trail. Especially as he might not be able to remember all the details now.

'That would really help me to know what to look out for,' she said.

'Mariana and I have been talking,' Angelo said. 'If she takes photographs on her computer, then you can sit down together, she can ask you questions about the paintings and you can tell her everything you remember. I'll translate for both of you.'

Leo patted his hand. 'That sounds like a good plan.'

'And we'll ship your paperwork back to London.'

'No,' Leo said. 'My papers stay in Florence.'

'Nonno, Mariana's studies are in London. We can't expect her to stay here for however long it takes to sort out the paperwork,' Angelo said gently. 'The papers will be at my house. That's almost the same as being yours.'

'No,' Leo said again.

Angelo glanced at Mariana. His expression said, *Leave it for now and I'll talk to him.*

'I can use online records as well,' Mariana said.

'What sort of records?' Angelo asked.

'Sales catalogues, inventories of artwork in private hands, diaries that mention paintings, mentions in wills, and a catalogue raisonné,' Mariana said, ticking them off on her fingers.

'I've never heard of a catalogue raisonné,' Angelo said.

'It's a list of all known artwork by a single artist. The one for Carulli might list sketches which are preparatory studies for Leo's paintings; or Leo's collection might have preparatory sketches for paintings that are listed in another collection,' she said. 'And sometimes there are historic photographs; they can show if a painting's been restored, altered or cut down.' She looked at Leo. 'Did you take photographs before your painting was restored?'

'Yes. I took photographs when I found the painting, too. They'll be in the boxes.'

'In colour?' she asked hopefully.

Leo smiled. 'I always liked my gadgets, so some will be in colour. Maybe there is cine film, too. Film of my Frederica.'

'My grandmother,' Angelo added softly for Mariana's benefit.

'Did she like art, too?'

'She was my model at art school,' Leo said. 'My father didn't approve. He wanted me to marry a banker's daughter, I guess to make up for the fact that I was never going to be a banker myself. But we married anyway. My father was angry for a while, but then Lucrezia came along and he fell in love with her. She followed him everywhere. And he was the one who discovered your mother could sing, right from when she was tiny. He found her the best singing tutor in Florence. And he had a seat right in the middle of the front row, every time she was on stage, until the day he died.'

'I've never heard that story before, Nonno,' Angelo said.

'We were so happy, Frederica and me. Angelo, I wish you and St—'

'Let's order coffee, Nonno,' Angelo cut in.

Mariana wondered what Leo had been about

to say. Had it been the beginning of someone's name? Angelo hadn't mentioned a partner, though surely as it was the weekend his partner would've joined them to visit Leo? The thinning of Angelo's lips warned her not to ask, which made her guess that it was a painful story. She didn't want to add to that hurt by asking personal and inappropriate questions, so she brought the conversation back to art. 'There is one other thing,' she said. 'If there are any gaps in ownership between 1933 and 1945, or there is a red-flag name in the list of previous owners, the art might need to be restored to its rightful owner.'

Leo's expression told her he knew exactly what she was alluding to. 'I bought *The Girl in the Window* in England,' he said. 'In 1963. It had been in the attic for years, which was how the mice got to it.'

After lunch, Mariana went back to her room to pick up her equipment, and called Nigel to fill him in on the situation and cancel their meeting on Monday. Back at the *palazzo*, she took a quick snap of each painting with her laptop, then sat down with Leo and Angelo at the dining room table.

'I'm going to record everything on my laptop so I can refer back to it, and then type up the notes,' she told Leo. 'I don't want to miss anything or forget anything.'

Leo patted her hand. 'At my age, dear child, you forget much. I can barely remember what we had for lunch just now. But I remember the past more clearly.'

'Good.' She smiled at him. 'Any time you want to stop for a rest, that's absolutely fine. We can take all the time you need.'

Angelo discovered that Mariana was as good as her word, making sure that Leo took breaks. And she was methodical as she went through each painting, letting Leo talk and reminisce but also making sure she got all the relevant bits of information so she could cross-check them at a later date with a paper trail. Clearly she'd interviewed a lot of people for her show and was experienced at making them relax while she got the information she needed.

Although Angelo was kept busy translating

between them, he still had time to notice little details about Mariana. The way she sat with head tilted slightly to one side as she listened; the way the sunlight through the window made her hair look the colour of a ripe cornfield; the way her lower lip was as full and lush and sensual as one of the models in his grandfather's paintings; the way the whole room felt as if it was filled with sunshine when she smiled.

He shook himself.

This was about Leo, not about his inappropriate attraction to Mariana Thackeray. He needed to keep his mind strictly on the job. Especially as he knew her past relationship had been so unhappy; she hadn't mentioned a partner who might resent her spending so much time with work, so he was guessing that she was single. Trusting someone after you'd been so badly let down was hard. And he came with baggage that she didn't need. Nothing could happen between them—except maybe a fling, and that felt unfair.

After dinner, Angelo walked her back to the hotel. 'I know you're perfectly capable of going on your own, but my grandfather has old-fashioned views and he'd be happier if I accompanied you,' he said.

He didn't say it, but Mariana guessed that he also wanted to talk to her without his grandfather overhearing.

Her suspicions were confirmed when he said, 'Thank you for being patient with Nonno. He's a bit intractable about his paperwork.'

'I like your grandfather very much,' she said. 'But we'll have a huge problem if he won't let you take the paperwork, because without that I can't sort out the provenance.'

'I'll talk him round. But it's a question of how we get it all to England. A courier won't touch it without an exact list of contents, and taking one box at a time as cabin baggage will take way too long.'

'So what are you thinking?' she asked. Angelo Beresford struck her as the kind of person who didn't bring up subjects without thinking about them deeply first.

'I'll hire a van and drive all the boxes back to London.'

'From Florence? But… Surely that'll take a couple of days?'

'I looked it up. The online travel guides say seventeen hours.'

'You can't drive for seventeen hours in a row!'

'Technically, I can,' he said. 'The legal time limits only apply to commercial vehicles.'

'In real terms, you'd be crazy. You'd be tired and you'd be a danger to other road users,' she pointed out.

'There might be an alternative,' he said, looking thoughtful. 'Do you have a driving licence?'

'Yes, but I've never driven abroad,' she said.

'Or driven a big van, I'm guessing?'

'No,' she confirmed.

'Then I won't ask you to drive. And you're right about tiredness. So we'll need to split the journey.' He took out his phone and flicked into the Internet. 'The halfway point is Dijon. If we leave on Friday morning, we'll be back in London on Saturday afternoon.'

'Angelo…'

'I know. It's longer than I asked you to be

here. But I think you're going to be the key to Nonno agreeing to let me take his papers. He knows you love art.'

'He knows you would take great care of his possessions.'

'But I don't feel the same way that he does about those paintings, and you do. That matters more to him. Please, Mariana. I need your help.'

Eric would have demanded.

Angelo had asked.

Politely.

He valued her knowledge. And he'd listened to her about the risk of driving from Florence to London in one go and changed his plan, rather than being pig-headed and sticking to his original intentions. She appreciated that.

'All right,' she said.

'Thank you.'

When they reached her hotel, Mariana paused in the lobby. 'Thank you for walking me back. I would invite you to have a drink with me, but I guess you need to get back to your grandfather.'

That gave them both a convenient excuse.

Even though she'd seen his professional accreditations and his protectiveness towards Leo showed that Angelo Moretti was one of the good guys, her experience with Eric had still left her wary. Eric had seemed so perfect at first; and her judgement couldn't have been more wrong. How could she be sure she'd get it right next time? Plus this was business. The attraction she felt towards Angelo had to be ignored. 'I'll see you tomorrow. What time would be best for Leo?'

'Half past eight?' he suggested.

'I'll be there. And thank you for translating today.'

'Any time.' He paused. 'If those journals are in his paperwork, then they'll be in Italian. I could translate them for you, which will help with speed, and then help you work your way through the rest of the papers.'

'Don't you have to be at the office?'

'I can delegate some work and do as much of the rest as possible from home. Right now Nonno is my priority.' He paused. 'While you're doing the photographs, I need to go up to Rome for the afternoon and see my sister. Is it OK to leave you with Nonno?'

'If he doesn't mind, it's fine.'

'Thank you.' He patted her shoulder. 'You're a kind woman. And my family appreciates what you're doing for us.'

Even though the touch of his hand was light and momentary, it sent a spark of desire through her and she found herself staring at his mouth. Wondering how it would feel against her skin. How it would feel if he wrapped his arms around her. Then she shook herself. No. This wasn't being professional. She needed to get a grip.

'See you tomorrow,' she said, cross at feeling so flustered. He was the first man to make her feel this way in a long time, and she really didn't know how to deal with it.

'Tomorrow,' he said.

Angelo was thoughtful all the way back to the *palazzo*.

Putting a hand momentarily on her shoulder had been a mistake. He was more aware of her then he had been of any woman since Stephanie, which was utterly ridiculous. His relationship with her should be strictly professional, simply to make his grandfather's dreams come true. Even though he knew she wasn't Stephanie, he also knew she'd been badly hurt in the past. And he was barely in the right place to deal with his own feelings, let alone anyone else's. He needed to back off.

Sunday was another day with Mariana listening to Leo telling her about the paintings; and on Monday morning she made a start on the more formal photography.

On Tuesday, Angelo headed to Rome. While on the train, he organised their return journey to London and emailed the details to Mariana, adding:

Send me a list of any stationery you need for London and I'll get it delivered.

Then he concentrated on catching up with emails from work and reassuring a couple of his clients before he arrived in Rome.

It didn't take long to reach the townhouse where his sister lived.

Eduardo, his brother-in-law, was at work—though, as it wasn't the end of the financial year, Angelo rather thought Ed might be trying to get some peace and quiet and using the excuse of being snowed under at the office. But his mother and sister greeted him warmly.

'Your favourites from London, Mamma,' he said, giving his mother a distinctive duck-egg-blue bag. She peered inside to discover a large box of her favourite tea and a jar of honey.

'Grazie.' She hugged him. 'You do spoil me.'

'And something for a new mother,' he said, handing Camilla a beautifully wrapped parcel. She opened it and beamed as she discovered luxury bubble bath, a scented candle and a box of chocolates.

'And I have something for my beautiful niece, too,' he said.

'She's asleep right now,' Camilla said, 'but I promise I'll wake her in an hour, when she's due a feed.'

'OK.' Giving him another hour to make sure his bravest face was in place, so his sister wouldn't be able to guess how much his heart ached. Because he absolutely wasn't going to let his personal pain spill over and hurt his family. 'I bought Ed some single malt to toast the baby, too.'

'You are *so* lovely.' Camilla hugged him. 'How's Nonno?'

'Very bright. Right now he's very happy, talking art all day to someone who actually appreciates it,' Angelo said.

'This art expert—she really knows her stuff?' Lucrezia demanded.

'Yes. She's currently taking professional photographs of all the paintings, and then she's going to work on Nonno's papers in London and sort them out properly.'

'He's letting you put them in order? But you and Cammie couldn't talk him into even touching them before, let alone taking them out of the *palazzo*.' Lucrezia looked surprised.

'He said no at first. But he realises that Mariana can't move to Florence for however long it takes to sort everything out, and the fact that she really loves his paintings means that he'll do it for her,' Angelo said. His grandfather was definitely falling under Mariana's spell—and Angelo had a nasty feeling that it would be very easy for him to do the same. 'We're driving them back to London on Friday.'

'*Driving?* Are you insane?' Camilla asked.

'We worked it out. It's the simplest way,' Angelo said.

'And she's nice?' Camilla asked.

Nice didn't even begin to cover it. But he didn't want to go there. Nothing could happen between them. He'd already learned the hard way that he wasn't husband material, and he was pretty sure that Mariana's own experiences had made her want to give relationships a wide berth, too. 'She knows a lot about art. And she loves her subject.' She *glowed* when she talked about the Macchiaioli painters, but how could he tell his mother and sister that without them getting the wrong idea? He knew they worried about him and wanted him to move on from Stephanie, but he just hadn't been able to. He couldn't face that kind of rejection again.

Mariana Thackeray wasn't the one to make him move on, either. He was sticking firmly with his career. Where his heart was safe. 'I think she'll do a good job,' he said. Best to keep it businesslike. And he really wanted to change the subject before his mother or his sister started asking awkward questions. 'Any chance of some coffee?' he asked plaintively.

Lucrezia made coffee, fussing over Camilla and insisting that she should put her feet up. And finally they heard a low cry.

The baby.

There was a huge difference between seeing a baby on a computer screen during a video call, and being in the same room as one. Mentally, Angelo locked away all the longing and the loneliness. This wasn't about him; it was about his sister and being able to make her feel all was right with the world. He'd managed to cope so far with the babies of friends—friends who didn't know exactly why Stephanie had divorced him.

But he wasn't prepared for the feelings that flooded through him when Camilla shyly put her daughter—his niece, his own flesh and blood—in his arms. A surge of love and tenderness that he'd never experienced before. Something that made the longing and the loneliness burn; yet, at the same time, this was so precious and special.

'Serafina Frederica,' he whispered.

She was two weeks old. She'd been born a month premature, so her skin was still wrinkly rather than plump, and her fingers were oh, so tiny.

'She's so like you, Cammie,' he said. 'I can see Ed in her, too, but she's the image of you. Just how I remember you being when I was five and Dad brought me to the hospital to meet you for the first time.'

Tears glittered in her eyes. 'Angelo—'

'She's gorgeous,' he said. 'My niece. I never expected...' He met his sister's gaze. 'I didn't expect her to make me feel like this. Proud and protective.' Even though it underlined what he'd never had, this was still something to be cherished. His niece. A baby whose life he'd be able to share, watch her grow up and love her more each day.

'Ed and I—we wondered if you'd—I know it's hard,' Camilla said.

'If I'd what?'

'You don't have to say yes, not if it's too much.' Camilla looked worried.

'Cammie, you're my baby sister and nothing is too much to ask,' he said gently.

She squirmed. 'Would you be her godfather?'

'Yes. Definitely yes.' He cradled his niece. He'd wanted a baby so much. He'd planned it all out in his head: he and Stephanie would have two or three children, a fluffy golden retriever, a garden full of laughter and sunshine at weekends. Stephanie had wanted that, too. It would've been perfect.

Except it hadn't happened, thanks to the mumps.

He pushed the thought away. Not now. He needed to focus on how lucky he was to have a grandfather and sister he adored, a mother he loved deeply even though her theatricality drove him a little crazy, a brother-in-law he liked and respected, and now tiny little Serafina. Being a godfather was the next best thing to being a father. Let love drown the sorrow.

And he already loved his niece. He noticed that her eyes had already changed from a newborn blue to a deep brown.

'So I'll be her godfather as well as her uncle,' he said. 'That's wonderful, Cammie. I'm so glad you asked me.'

'Really?'

'Really,' he confirmed. 'I'm not just saying it. I'm—' His voice sounded slightly choked. 'I'm honoured. Delighted. It's… It's the closest I'll get to being a dad, and I… Thank you.'

There were tears in her eyes. 'I don't want to hurt you, Angelo.'

'I'm not hurt,' he fibbed, stuffing down the heartache. 'I'm just so glad. I love you, Cammie. And I love my niece. My goddaughter-to-be.'

Unexpectedly, he found himself thinking of Mariana. Did she have any nieces or nephews? Was she close to them? *Did she want children of her own?*

But that question could open up his world of bleakness again. He needed to keep that locked away. Focus on what he could have, not what he couldn't.

'We'll let your *mamma* feed you, *mimma*,' he said softly, handing the baby back. 'And then your *mamma* can open my present to you and I'll read you the first story from it. When you're older, you'll love the pictures. Maybe you'll be like your *nonna* and your *bisnonno* and appreciate art, unlike your Zio Angelo.'

Again, tears glistened in Camilla's eyes. 'Angelo, this means so m—'

'I know,' he cut in gently. 'I was always going to love her, Cammie.' Always. Even though his heart ached and wished that he, too, had a baby to share his family's love. Focus on the good. Don't focus on what they couldn't have. Be grateful for the very, very good things they already had: their family.

'Come and help me with the washing up, Angelo,' Lucrezia directed when Camilla was settled on the sofa and feeding the baby.

Angelo followed his mother into the kitchen, but before she could say anything he gave her a hug. 'I'm fine, Mamma. Don't worry. I'm over it.' It wasn't true, but there was nothing to achieve by dwelling on it and going over and over things that couldn't be changed. 'I'm really happy for Cammie and Ed.'

Lucrezia hugged him back. 'I know, but—'

'But nothing, Mamma,' he cut in gently. 'Everything is just fine.' And it would be. He'd make it happen.

He stayed for dinner so he had a chance to see his brother-in-law and congratulate him on the baby, too. And leaving Serafina was a real wrench. By the time Angelo got back to Florence, Mariana had gone back to her hotel and Leo had gone to bed. Angelo showered and went to bed, but it was a long time before he could sleep. Seeing his niece had unsettled him, awoken longings he'd have to fight to bury again. His growing attraction towards Mariana had unsettled him, too. But he needed to be careful with her. She'd had a horrible time with her ex. The last thing she needed was to get involved with him. If she wanted a family of her own—he couldn't give her that, so it was better not to start anything in the first place.

He needed to keep his distance. Keep things professional. He'd managed that with every other relationship in the last couple of years, being charming at dinner parties when he'd been invited as the 'eligible single' while making it clear that his career kept him too busy to date anyone properly. Why was it so much more of a struggle to maintain that distance with Mariana? Why was he even thinking about finding out how she felt, if she might be prepared to take a chance on him? Why couldn't he think of her as dispassionately as he had about every other woman he'd met since his marriage ended?

On Wednesday, the rest of the boxes arrived, and Angelo packed everything into them. About the only order he managed to restore to the chaos was to put the journals together, along with some reels of cine films that he planned to have transferred to a digital format once he was back in London. There was no clue as to the content of the films, just a couple of years written on the outside—years when his grandparents had been newlyweds and his mother had been a small child, and he thought both his grandfather and his mother would enjoy seeing them.

But then he found some preparatory sketches that looked vaguely familiar, and took them out to Mariana to see what she thought.

'That's absolutely incredible!' she said, her eyes glittering as she inspected them. 'They're dated and signed, and, look, there's a note in Carulli's own handwriting about the location. This is fantastic!'

She threw her arms round him and hugged him.

For a second, Angelo froze and panic flooded through him. Distance, he reminded himself. *Distance.*

But his body wasn't listening to his head, and he wrapped his arms round her. This felt so *right.* He closed his eyes and dipped his head slightly to press his cheek against hers, breathing in the clean vanilla scent of her hair. A warmth, a closeness he hadn't felt since Stephanie had walked out on him.

Then reality washed back in.

This was the last thing he should be doing.

So much for keeping things professional.

He released her and took a step backwards.

And then she flushed. 'Sorry, I got a bit carried away just then. The excitement of finding the artwork.'

'Me, too,' he lied. It hadn't been the artwork.

As far as he was concerned, the sketch was nothing special. It didn't make his heart beat faster. That reaction had all been because of *her*.

Not that he was going to make the mistake of telling her that.

'I know which painting it is.' She flicked into the photos she'd downloaded to her laptop the previous day. 'You can see the cottage here, and this group of trees. It ties up.'

'So we're getting somewhere,' he said.

At least, as far as his grandfather's paintings were concerned. Where his heart was concerned, he needed to get a grip. He hadn't been enough for Stephanie and he had no intention of putting himself in a place where he discovered that he wasn't enough for Mariana, either.

The fact that his heart felt as if it had done an anatomically impossible backflip every time she smiled or he looked into her blue, blue eyes—well, he'd have to learn to ignore it.

CHAPTER FOUR

ON THURSDAY, MARIANA finished photographing the paintings, and Angelo had pretty much finished putting everything into the boxes.

'We could,' Mariana suggested, 'go to the Pitti Palace.'

'And see the Macchiaioli paintings,' Leo said, looking animated.

'Provided we get a taxi, Nonno,' Angelo cut in. 'We're not walking from here, not on a hot afternoon. It will tire Mariana too much.'

For a second, she looked as if she was going to argue, but then she clearly realised what he was doing. Giving his grandfather an excuse to keep his dignity. 'Being English, I find the heat too much,' she said. 'But a nice quiet afternoon in a cool art gallery...'

Angelo gave her a grateful smile, appreciating the fact she was putting his grandfather first.

At the Pitti Palace Angelo let most of their chat about the art go over his head, though he enjoyed seeing his grandfather so lively as they looked round the gallery. Mariana, too; she held the old man's arm and supported him while making it look as if she was the one who wanted support, and she and Leo were almost gleeful as they talked about details of each painting. Every so often, she caught his gaze and her eyes crinkled at the corners. How could she have no idea how gorgeous she was?

Well, he knew the answer to that. Her ex had clearly damaged her confidence. But the more Angelo saw of Mariana, the more he liked her. The more he felt drawn to her. And when they'd held each other for that brief moment yesterday… Had it been simply the thrill of discovery carrying her away, or did she, too, feel that draw between them? Could they take a risk on each other? Or would he just be setting himself up for heartache?

On Friday, after the van arrived, Mariana checked out of her hotel and came to pick up her equipment, and she helped to load the van with the boxes.

'You will come back again to see me, Mariana?' Leo asked, holding her close.

'Of course. And I'll send you daily updates about the work I'm doing,' she promised.

'But I don't have a computer,' he said.

'But I do,' Lucia said. 'Send the updates to me, and come back soon.'

'Thank you for looking after me so well,' Mariana said.

Angelo hugged his grandfather. 'I'll be back soon,' he promised.

And please, please let the excitement about the art stay with Leo for a little longer. Keep him going. Keep him *alive*. Angelo wasn't ready to lose his grandfather yet.

'I did wonder if I was going to have to navigate,' Mariana said as Angelo drove them out of Florence.

'Don't speak too soon. If anything goes wrong with the satnav, then you might have to,' he said.

'You'd trust me to map-read?' she asked.

He glanced at her in surprise. 'Of course.'

'Thank you.'

It was obvious that her ex had dented her

confidence, but Angelo didn't want to make her feel awkward about it. 'You strike me as being a very capable woman,' he said.

'That's kind of you.'

'It wasn't meant to be kind, more a statement of fact,' he said. 'Talking of kind—Nonno's really brightened, this week, thanks to you.'

'I'm glad. I know how it feels when your grandfather is sick and it's not something that can be held at bay for long, and the only thing you can do is try to make their days a bit happier. I'm just glad I can help—though I admit I'm also really thrilled to be working on paintings that nobody except your grandfather has seen for years.'

'The thrill of discovery?'

'That—and also Carulli is my favourite painter.'

'The best of both worlds, then.' He paused. 'Forgive me for asking—but how did you cope when you lost your grandfather?'

'Pretty badly,' she said. 'Grandad was the only one who saw through Eric—my ex—and wasn't hoodwinked by his charm. And I miss him. I miss chatting to him. I miss him singing the Beatles and the Beach Boys songs he taught my sister and me when I was tiny. I guess he's still here, in a way, because he's always in our hearts, and those memories will always be here. But I wish he was still here in person to see that I've come out the other side of my—well,' she said. 'That I'm not letting what happened with Eric drag me down and I'm getting on with my life.'

Exactly what Angelo knew his own grandfather wanted him to do. Move on. But how could he be sure that, if he tried again, he wouldn't end up hitting the same problem and being rejected for the same reason that Stephanie had dumped him?

'I'm sure he knows,' Angelo said. 'There are more things in heaven and earth, and all that.'

She smiled. 'Now that I wasn't expecting—for you to quote *Hamlet* at me.'

'It was my A level text,' he said.

'So you like the theatre?'

'I don't go that often.' He pretty much buried himself in work. 'Between Italy and work, I don't have the time.'

'Didn't you think about working in Italy

rather than London, so you don't have to spend so much time travelling?' she asked.

'I grew up in London,' he said. 'So did Cammie. She moved to Rome three years ago because that's where Ed—her husband—is based.'

'I meant to ask you how your sister and the baby were doing,' she said. 'Sorry for being rude. I guess it slipped my mind because I was so caught up in the paintings.'

'They're fine,' he said. He really didn't want to talk about the baby—because the next question would be all too obvious. Using a closed answer instead of giving details would mean she wouldn't ask.

But she didn't take the hint. Instead, she opened up the conversation. 'It's nice having a baby in the family,' she said. 'I have a nephew—my older sister Sophie's son, Olly. He's five.'

Just what he'd wondered when he was in Rome. He couldn't help asking, 'And you're close?'

'I am now,' she said quietly.

'Now?' The question was out before he could stop it, even though he knew it was intrusive.

'I see him every weekend and I have a regular Wednesday night babysitting slot—it means Sophie and Laurence can have a date night, and I get to read all my favourite children's books to Olly and play with his train set.'

It was the *now* that bugged him. Why hadn't she been close to her nephew before? He couldn't imagine Mariana falling out badly with anyone. She was sweet and kind. So had it been her ex making her keep her distance?

'Eric—my ex—didn't like it if I spent too much time with Sophie and Olly,' she said, confirming his guess.

'Because he didn't like children?'

'Partly because he needed to keep me isolated, so I'd believe everything he told me— but partly because he didn't like children,' she said. 'When we first met, he gave me the impression that he wanted to settle down and have a family, but that was obviously part of the charm to draw me in because he knew I wanted children.'

She wanted children.

Exactly what he couldn't give her. How stupid he'd been to let himself get distracted by his feelings and start to wonder if things could work out between them. Of course they couldn't.

It felt as if a huge weight was dragging him down to the bottom of the sea and Angelo missed what she said next, but he forced himself to concentrate.

'He said he wasn't quite ready because things were crazy at work, and suggested putting it off for a year. But then, when the other side of him came out...' She lifted one shoulder in a weary shrug. 'By the time he'd finished, I thought I'd be the most useless mother in the world anyway so it wouldn't be fair to have a child.'

Even though this was trampling on his sorest spot, Angelo couldn't stand by and let her believe that. 'Of course you wouldn't be a useless mother. It sounds as if you're a wonderful aunt.'

'There's a big difference between looking after a child for a few hours and being there full-time.'

'True, but being there for some of the time is still good practice.' It was like picking at a scab, but he had to say it. 'I hope what Eric said hasn't squashed your dreams.'

'No. It's just—well, meeting someone. It's hard. Where do you meet someone of your own age if not through work?'

'Friends fixing you up—or dating websites,' he said.

She grimaced. 'If it was a friend of a friend, maybe. But not a dating site. I don't think you can get a good idea of what someone is really like through a computer screen.'

Was that how she'd met her ex? It would be cruel to ask. But, as if she guessed what he was thinking, she said, 'I met Eric at a party. A friend of a friend of a friend.'

'Ah. So he should have been safe.'

She nodded. 'Except he wasn't. I guess you only ever know what a person is really like when you're in a relationship with them.'

'Not necessarily. They might be a bit more open with a partner than they would be with a colleague or friend, or maybe less shy at home, but their basic personality is surely the same?'

'So how,' she asked, 'did I get it so wrong with Eric?'

He thought about it. 'Maybe he's the rare exception that proves the rule. You said he charmed your family and friends as well.'

'Except my grandad.' She sighed again. 'It's going to take a while before I can trust my judgement again. I know my parents and my sister and my friends want me to move on, but it's hard.'

Tell me about it, he thought. 'Maybe,' he said, 'you should cut yourself some slack. You weren't the only one taken in by him.'

'I guess.' She shrugged. 'But I don't think I'd trust a dating website and most of the people I meet are already involved with someone, or they've got baggage.' She grimaced. 'Which is hypocritical of me, because I have baggage, too.'

'You'll meet someone,' he said, and squashed the thought that she already had—she'd met him. Because, even though he was attracted to her, what she'd just told him put a very different light on things. Wanting children meant that he'd be out of the equation as a potential partner because he couldn't give her what she wanted—just as he'd failed Stephanie.

'What about you?' she asked. 'Do you want children at some point?'

It was a question he didn't want to answer. Because then he'd have to explain about the mess of his past, and he really didn't want to have to face her pity. 'I'm pretty busy with my job,' he said instead.

Or maybe it would be better to tell a slight untruth to deflect any questions. 'That's why I'm divorced, actually. My ex wanted children.'

That was true, up to a point. But he knew Mariana would infer from what he'd just said that the reason they were divorced was because his ex had wanted children and he hadn't, rather than the real scenario: that he couldn't have them naturally and his ex didn't want to consider the alternatives. Stephanie had wanted a baby of her own, with no complications. She hadn't been willing to compromise. And it had left him feeling completely inadequate. He wasn't going to put himself in the position where that could happen again.

'Uh-huh,' Mariana said.

He gave her a sidelong glance. It looked as if she'd processed the information exactly as he'd planned and thought that he didn't want children of his own. And why would you get involved with someone who wanted the opposite from life that you did, especially if your ex had treated you as badly as Eric had treated her? That put him safely off limits.

They stopped at Milan to grab a sandwich and coffee, headed up through to Chamonix and Geneva, and finally reached Dijon.

Mariana helped to shift all the boxes to their rooms—Angelo didn't want to leave them on the van overnight—and then they went to the restaurant for a quick dinner.

'You look shattered,' she said.

He brushed it aside. 'I'm fine.'

But his dreams that night were filled with visions of Mariana laughing and looking happy, and when he woke he was filled with longing. Oh, for pity's sake. What was the point of wanting something you couldn't have?

But he schooled himself to be nice and let her chatter to him about art all the way through breakfast and the next leg of their drive through France.

'So what's your grand career plan?' he asked.

'When I've finished my PhD? I'd like to keep working on *Hidden Treasure* for as long as the programme runs. I'd like to teach part-time. And I'd love to work on Carulli's catalogue raisonné and update it, once we've sorted out your grandfather's paperwork.' She paused. 'Why? Were you going to offer me a job?'

'Setting up the gallery? To be honest, I haven't thought that far ahead,' he said. 'My focus is on getting that painting authenticated, so Nonno can—' He stopped abruptly.

Die happy. Mariana knew what Angelo wasn't saying, and how much it must be hurting him. She'd been there herself. She reached over and laid her hand briefly on his in a gesture of fellow feeling. 'I'm sorry. I know how hard it is, watching someone you love fade and not being able to do anything. Though you *are* doing something for your grandfather. You're giving him vindication, and I promise I'll do my best to help you.'

'Is that why you do *Hidden Treasure*?' he asked.

She nodded. 'It's not very nice on the occasions when we have to disappoint people, but most of the people on the show don't care about the monetary value of the artwork. It's about having their painting accepted by the experts—some of whom can be really stuffy. I guess it's kind of helping the underdog, and that's really satisfying.' She paused. 'What about you?'

'My grand career plan? I'm a partner now, so I guess I'm working towards being a senior partner. I like what I do. It's about fairness and making sure any employees get looked after properly if the firm they work for is merged with another or bought out.'

'So you tend to work for the underdog, too,' she said.

'In a way,' he agreed.

Mariana was still on her quest to get to know him better. He'd told her almost nothing about himself. She knew he was divorced, and it had clearly been messy because he avoided talking about it. He didn't want children. So what did he want? she wondered. What made his heart beat faster? His work? 'Did you always want to be a lawyer?' she asked.

'Just like my dad. Yes.' He smiled. 'Dad was your archetypal quiet and serious lawyer. He and Mamma were complete opposites—but I think he made her feel grounded, and she... Well, he always said he fell in love with her voice. He'd gone to the opera for a corporate thing, and expected to hate it—but it was the *Flute*. Mamma's famous for her role as the Queen of the Night. There was a party afterwards, he met her along with the rest of the cast, and he proposed a week later at sunset at the top of Primrose Hill.'

'That's so romantic,' she said. 'My parents knew each other from school, but didn't really notice each other until Dad came home from his first time at university. It was a New Year party, and they ended up kissing at midnight.' She smiled. 'They still hold hands, and they've been married for forty years.'

'That's nice.' For a second, he looked incredibly sad.

She remembered what he'd said about his ex. Did he miss her? Was he still in love with her? But their differences over wanting children had clearly been too huge for them to overcome. And it was none of her business. She shouldn't ask.

Though it was also a warning not to get the wrong idea about him. Angelo Beresford was a very attractive man—and he was a good man, too. Kind. It would be oh, so easy to fall for him, but it would also be a huge mistake. She wanted children one day and he didn't. There wasn't a middle way. If they fell for each other, they'd just end up making each other unhappy. So she'd stick to being professional and keep a tiny bit of distance between them.

'So what does a corporate lawyer do for fun?' she asked. 'Music? Cinema? Sport?'

'Between work and my family, I don't have much time for hobbies,' he said.

Because he was a workaholic? She could identify with that. She'd thrown herself into her studies and her job, to prove to herself that she was so much more than Eric had made her believe she was. 'Your mum's an opera singer. Do you like classical music more than pop?'

'A mix.' He gave her a sidelong look. 'When

I went through the rebellious teenage stage, I listened to terrible music. You know, the stuff that's little more than fuzzy noise and guitar solos played as fast as possible.' He grinned. 'Mamma retaliated by singing the arias with the most dramatic scales and runs, to prove her music was faster and louder and much more technically challenging than the guitar solos I listened to.'

She laughed. 'Your mum sounds amazing. And you've seen her sing on stage?'

'In all the major roles. Mamma's a dramatic coloratura soprano, so she played the big tragic parts. Norma, Lucia, Aida—and obviously the Queen of the Night.' He paused. 'What about you? What does an art expert do for fun?'

'Visit art galleries,' she said promptly. 'Though I love cinema, especially period dramas.'

'And you spend half your time spotting the artwork in it?'

'Absolutely—that's the best bit,' she said with a smile. 'There was a series set in Florence and I drove my sister potty by picking out all the sculptures and frescoes. Though it's so good spending time with her.'

Angelo was guiltily aware that he hadn't spent enough time with his sister since her pregnancy and Serafina's birth. But, now he'd overcome that first hurdle, he'd make more effort. 'I'm glad that your ex didn't ruin things completely.'

'Sophie could see what he was doing, fairly early on—but at the time I was still blinded by his charm and I kind of played into his hands,' she said. 'But when my mum and my best friend twigged as well, they joined her in trying to help me and they refused to give up on me. I'm really grateful for my family.'

'I'm sure you would've done the same for them if it had been the other way round,' he said.

'Of course. They're all pushing me to date again,' she admitted. 'But it's hard to trust. I got it so wrong last time—how do I know I won't make the same mistake again?'

He knew how that felt. He'd picked the wrong person, too—though if it hadn't been for that bout of mumps things might have been so very different. If they'd been able to have a baby, maybe their marriage would've stood a chance. 'I guess you just have to take that first difficult step,' he said, knowing that he was being a complete hypocrite because he had no intention of doing that himself.

'I'm happy with my work,' she said.

'Me, too.'

She raised an eyebrow. 'Is your family trying to encourage you to date, too?'

'I don't have time, between work and Nonno.'

The way she shifted in her seat told him she recognised that for the feeble excuse it was. 'You mean, you don't want to take the risk.'

'No.' And he didn't. If anyone could've tempted him, it would've been Mariana Thackeray, with those stunning blue eyes and that sensual curve to her mouth—but she wanted children. He already knew from her profile on the television studio's website that she was four years younger than him, almost at the age where her biological clock would start ticking. And that was an area where he definitely couldn't deliver. What was the point of disappointing them both?

Finally they reached Calais, got onto the train to get through the tunnel, and at last back to London. He insisted on dropping her at home; apart from the fact he'd taken up so much of her time, he wanted to put some distance between them. Some of their conversations had made him antsy and he needed to get his equilibrium back. Unloading the boxes and moving things about made him physically tired enough to block out the questions in his head and let him sleep.

On Monday morning, Mariana turned up at Nigel's office at half past eight with a turmeric latte and a muffin.

'This had *better* be good, getting me here for the crack of dawn,' he grumbled.

She laughed, knowing he was teasing. 'It is.' She showed him the photographs she'd taken. 'I sent these to Jeremy and he rang me up and practically asked me to marry him.'

'It'd never work. You're missing a Y-chromosome, and besides I think Bernie would have something to say about you marrying his husband,' Nigel said with a grin.

She grinned. 'You know what I mean. And we have paperwork. I don't know exactly what's there, but there are journals. Angelo is going to translate them while I sort through everything else. And hopefully we'll get to the bottom of this painting. I'd stake my flat on it being a genuine Carulli. But I want to know what it was doing in an attic, nibbled by mice. It's gorgeous. Why didn't they hang it in the house?'

'Find the story,' Nigel said.

'Even if it doesn't end up in the show, I still need to know,' she said. 'Look at the light. The way he painted her.'

'It reminds me a bit of *Beata Beatrix*,' he said. 'Rossetti's memorial to his wife. The light on her face is transcendent.'

'She's so beautiful,' Mariana said softly. '*The Girl in the Window*. I want to know who she is and what's her story.'

'Go get 'em, tiger,' Nigel said.

When she left the office, Mariana headed for Bloomsbury. Angelo's house was in a beautiful square: a gorgeous four-storey Georgian place with the first storey painted white, the rest in yellow brick, with dormer windows in a slate roof. There were huge sash windows, an ornate fanlight over the solid black front door, wrought iron railings at the front, and a bay tree in a square pewter pot on the front steps.

She rang the doorbell; when Angelo opened the door, her mouth went dry.

He looked even more formidable than usual in a business suit, crisp white shirt and understated silk tie, and she wished she'd worn a suit instead of her casual jeans and a T-shirt. Right now, she felt completely out of place.

'Thank you for coming,' he said, his expression polite and inscrutable. 'Come in.'

The entrance hall looked as if it had the original cornicing; stairs led up to the next floor, and the flooring was black and white tiling. There was a gilded mirror positioned artfully to reflect the light, and a marble-topped occasional table beneath it holding an orchid in a plain white pot. The walls were painted cream, and she was a little surprised to see that there was no art whatsoever on the walls. Given that every space possible in Leo's rooms had been crammed with paintings, this felt austere in the extreme.

'I'll give you the guided tour,' he said. 'The cloakroom is here on the left. And here's the dining room, which I've moved around so there's space to store all my grandfather's things, plus there's a table if you need to spread anything out.'

'Thank you. Is that where I'll be working?'

'No—that's the next floor up. I've made space for you in my office. If we bring one box up at a time to work on, it'll be less over-whelming,' he said.

That was thoughtful. She peered into the room and saw that the boxes were all neatly stacked.

'Shall we pick the top one and start on that?' she asked.

'Yes. I've already fished out the journals— I put them to one side as I came across them when I was packing. I think we've got a com-plete set, though there might be a couple miss-ing. I made a start on the translation while you were in your meeting this morning.'

'Don't start at the beginning,' she said. 'I

know we need to do all of them eventually, but you said you wanted to start with *The Girl in the Window* and get that authenticated. Leo said he bought the painting in 1963, so if we allow a few years either side just in case he's misremembered over the years, maybe you can see if you can find any information from 1960 to 1966?'

'Good idea. OK. This is the living room,' he said, indicating another door on her left. She didn't quite dare to peek inside. If it wasn't connected to work, she'd consider it out of bounds. She wasn't going to pry.

'Kitchen,' he said, leading her into the room at the end of the hallway.

She loved the room—bright, airy and full of light. Clearly it had been extended because the back wall was pure glass, looking out onto a patio which held large pewter pots filled with lavender. There was a table and chairs next to the glass wall; the cabinets in the rest of the room were all of pale wood, with granite worktops and a slate floor, and the walls were painted sage green. Nothing was out of place; there were no cookery books or magazines scattered on a countertop or the table, no mugs in the sink or on the draining board, and it looked more like a show kitchen than a working one. Then again, Angelo had told her that he liked everything in its right place. The only things on the countertop were a kettle and an expensive-looking coffee-maker.

'We're working on the next floor.' He ushered her towards the stairs. Again, there were no paintings on the walls or in the hallway upstairs. She would definitely have had artwork on these walls. The light was fabulous. How could he live in a world with no paintings, when his grandfather was a collector and his mother was an opera singer? Unless his ex had been a painter; but that felt too intrusive to ask.

'Another living room,' he said, gesturing to a room on the right, 'and this is my study.'

Like the other rooms she'd seen, it appeared to have original cornicing. There was a white Adam fireplace with a black-leaded grate, and a mirror on the wall over it to reflect the light from the window; adjacent to the fireplace was a wall full of bookshelves; and between them were two tables with an office chair each. One was completely clear, with a box of the stationery she'd asked for at the side, and the other held a phone, a computer and reading lamp.

The difference between the cluttered study in Leo's *palazzo* and his grandson's minimalist townhouse couldn't have been more stark.

Again, there was no artwork on the walls: just a very functional clock.

He gestured to the table. 'I hope that's satisfactory.'

'I think,' she said, 'I'd almost be afraid to put a single piece of paper on that table.'

He frowned. 'How else are you meant to sort through Nonno's papers?'

She nodded at his desk. He'd warned her that he was the only teenage boy who never had to be yelled at to tidy his room, but this went way beyond tidy. 'Are you sure you won't mind me breaching your clear desk policy?'

'It's your project. Run it as you wish.' His voice was expressionless, and she made a mental note to make absolutely sure that her desk was clear at the end of each day.

'I plan to focus on helping you go through

the paperwork, but I might need to take some calls from the office,' Angelo said. 'Obviously I trust that you'll keep anything you overhear in strictest confidence.'

'Of course. But I can work with headphones on, if you prefer.'

He shook his head. 'That won't be necessary. I know you'll keep your word.'

'Right.' She took a deep breath. 'I have a meeting with my tutor every Wednesday morning and with Nigel on Friday afternoons, and if Nigel needs me to go into the studios I'll let you have as much notice as possible. Other than that, I'll try to work the same hours that you do.'

He grimaced. 'Please don't feel that I'm going to be a slave driver. This is your area of expertise, not mine—run the project as you see fit.'

'We have a ticking clock,' she said gently, not wanting to hurt him by referring to his grandfather's condition, but wanting to reassure him that she understood the urgency. 'And I love my job. Working the necessary hours to get the job done on time isn't a problem.'

'Thank you,' he said. 'Shall I bring the first box up for you?'

'That would be kind.' She paused. 'The journal translations—if you can make a timeline as you go, that would be helpful. A note of the date, the artwork he bought, the artist's name, as much detail as he gives in the journal—any descriptions, measurements, sizes, price and what have you—and a note of the year of the journal and the page number of the entry.'

'Right.'

He looked slightly offended, and Mariana remembered that he was a partner in a legal firm. At a very young age. Meaning that he was more than bright enough to work it out for himself.

She must've flinched, because Angelo said, 'I'm sorry. Of course you know what information you're looking for to tie in with the other records. I didn't mean to snap at you.'

Eric never apologised, and the simple courtesy made Mariana feel as if she could breathe again.

'I guess I'm used to being the bossy one as

well as a neat freak,' Angelo said. 'When Dad died, ten years ago, Cammie was in the last year of her degree, Mamma fell apart completely and I was the one who held everything together. It's become kind of a habit to be in charge.'

'Well, they are *your* family papers.'

'And you're the expert I hired to make some sense of them,' he said.

Which made their relationship very clear. He was her client. Off limits.

Mariana worked quietly and methodically, Angelo discovered during the rest of the morning. He'd hardly know that he was sharing his office space—apart from the fact that he was incredibly aware of her. And he found himself glancing up from his own work to watch her. The tiny pleat between her eyebrows when she was concentrating; the way she tucked a strand of hair behind her ear; the way her glasses slipped down to the end of her nose over the course of a few minutes and then she pushed them back again.

He really shouldn't let himself get distracted.

But he couldn't help it. Something about Mariana Thackeray drew him.

There couldn't be any future in this. He wasn't looking for a relationship and she was obviously very focused on her studies and her work. She'd told him that she wanted kids. It could never work between them. But, even though he knew the sensible thing would be to ignore his burgeoning feelings, he caught himself thinking, *What if...?*

He checked his emails from the office, made a couple of phone calls and then went back to working on journal transcriptions. Before he realised it, it was gone one o'clock. Whatever her usual schedule was, he was aware that she was still working through the papers—trying not to disturb him, perhaps?

'Shall we have a break for lunch?' he asked.

She looked up from her desk. 'OK.'

He tried to put himself in her shoes. 'Please feel free to have a break whenever you need one. And help yourself to whatever you want from the fridge.'

'Thank you.'

Her polite smile told him she had no intention of taking him up on the offer. Did he really make people feel that awkward? Or did she have a filter in her head that made her judge other people by her ex's behaviour?

'Come to the kitchen and I'll show you how to use the coffee machine—it's a bit temperamental.' He led the way down to the kitchen, set out the food and the plates, then dealt with the coffee machine.

'Thank you. This all looks very nice, but I really don't expect you to provide lunch every day,' she said.

'The very least I can do is to feed you while you're here,' he said. 'My family would be appalled if I didn't. I might be half-English, but I feed people like an Italian—it's how I grew up. Is there anything you don't eat?'

She smiled. 'No allergies, and no food dislikes to worry about.'

'That makes life easy, then.'

'Your garden is lovely,' she said when they sat down to eat.

He barely noticed it; he simply paid his cleaner to do a bit of weeding and water the tubs of flowers. Rosie enjoyed gardening, and particularly liked the free rein he gave her when it came to planting. 'Thank you,' he said. 'How's it going?'

'I'm logging receipts on the spreadsheet and cross-referencing them to the files for each painting as I come across them. I've found some things relating to a couple of the paintings, but nothing so far on *The Girl in the Window.*'

They reached for a piece of bread at the same time and their fingers brushed; she drew back as if she'd been burned.

'Sorry,' he said.

'My fault.' She flushed.

He needed to put space between them, so she didn't feel uncomfortable with him. 'I'm going back to my desk,' he said. 'But feel free to take as long a break as you need.'

She seemed to have composed herself by the time she came back into his office.

'I've got some information from the journal in 1962 that you might find interesting,' he said. 'Nonno bought a small landscape by Carulli from a dealer.'

'1962? Give me a second.' She retrieved her laptop and tapped into a file. 'Here we go. He told me he bought this one in Florence. Hopefully the dealer's receipt, which might list the provenance, will be in one of the boxes, but the records for this particular dealer have been digitised, so I can check online to see when the dealer bought it, who from, and we can trace it from there.'

'I'm beginning to understand why your audience likes this sort of thing. It's finding all the bits of the puzzle and putting them together,' Angelo said.

'And they get the speeded-up version, so they don't have to wait to find the pieces,' she said with a smile. 'Though I admit I love this work. I've found some sketches and etchings, so I'm making a separate list of them.'

'This is really going to happen, isn't it?'

She nodded. 'We'll get his full collection catalogued.' She took a deep breath. 'This isn't a tactful question, but I need to ask. That ticking clock. How long do we have?'

'Months, if we're lucky.'

'But you don't think we have that long.'

'No. The specialist admitted it was more likely to be weeks. Six or seven at best.' And he hated the thought of losing his grandfather. He hated what it would do to his mother and his sister, too.

She went over to him then, and rested her hand on his shoulder. 'I'm sorry. It must be so hard for you. I was really close to my grandfather, too, and when he was diagnosed with dementia it was difficult for all of us. Sometimes he'd be bright; sometimes he wouldn't know who we were. Sometimes it'd change in the middle of a visit—he'd be chatting to me and then suddenly he'd look lost and the light would be gone from his eyes. Seeing him suffer was horrible. But I wouldn't have missed a single visit, because I knew that having company made his day that little bit brighter. So I kind of understand how it is for you. A long goodbye, where you're not ready to lose them and you really don't want them to go, but at the same time you don't want them to suffer and you want it to be over so they're at peace.'

'Yes.' He reached up to put his hand over hers. 'That's exactly it. Thank you for understanding.'

For a second, there was something he couldn't quite read in her expression. Something he didn't dare let himself think about. 'We'd better get on,' he said, trying to keep it brisk and businesslike.

Later that afternoon, she came over to his desk again, with her laptop. 'Would you mind just checking this for me, please?' she asked.

It was an email to Lucia, asking her to pass on an update to Leo. It was written in very simple Italian, saying that they'd been through three of the diaries and had a list of artwork to look out for, and they'd found references to six of the paintings so far. She'd also found some sketches, and she enclosed a couple of pictures for him.

'That's really kind of you,' Angelo said. 'And I'm impressed you've written in Italian.'

'It's a bit schoolgirly, but I wanted to make the effort.'

'That's the key thing,' he said gently. 'And your Italian is just fine.'

'I'll send it now. I've backed up all my files.' She handed him a flash drive. 'And this is your copy. I'll update this every day.'

'Thank you.' He glanced at the clock. 'I didn't realise how late it was.'

'I got caught up in my work. Sorry. I shouldn't impose.'

'Please, don't apologise.' And he didn't like that brief flicker of wariness in her eyes. Was she afraid of him? But, if so, why? Was it to do with her ex? And why did she apologise so much? 'Don't feel you have to work ridiculous hours,' he said. 'And would you like to stay for dinner?'

'Thank you for the offer, but my mum is expecting me,' she said.

Though she didn't meet his eyes, so he was pretty sure that was a polite fiction.

'Can I bring my easel and lights tomorrow,

so they're ready when I need to take photographs of any artwork?' she asked.

'Of course,' he said.

'See you tomorrow,' she said. 'Goodnight.'

CHAPTER FIVE

PROFESSIONAL. THAT WAS what she needed to be, Mariana thought. Instead of the jeans and T-shirt she usually wore when she was studying or working off-camera, she dressed in a dark grey business suit, a white shirt and black high-heeled shoes.

She was glad she'd opted for formality when Angelo opened the door to her, wearing another formal business suit. He had to be the only person she'd ever met who dressed like that when working from home. And, now she thought of it, he'd worn a suit in Florence, too. Most people dressed casually for visiting family and Angelo was definitely close to his grandfather. Why the formality? she wondered. Was it a way of putting a little bit of distance between him and the world?

'Let me help you with those,' he said.

'I'm fine,' she said.

'Are you telling me you hauled all that lot on the tube this morning?' he asked, eyeing the bag she was carrying with her easel, tripod and a photographic light, as well as her camera and her laptop.

'No. I took a taxi,' she said. But she let him take the easel and the tripod from her and carry them into the dining room.

'Good,' he said. 'I'll reimburse you for the fare.'

She spent the morning going through the second box and making notes. Angelo made them lunch again, and she made a mental note to bring muffins on Thursday morning. She wanted to make a contribution rather than feeling as if she was taking all the time.

'From the amount of photocopying you did this morning, I assume it's going well,' he said.

'Very much.' She smiled at him. 'My tutor— the one supervising my PhD—would quite like to meet you. Would that be possible?'

'As Leo's representative, you mean? Yes,' he said.

'And I had a very quick look through the

rest of the boxes. I'd like to get some archive-quality plastic pockets and acid-free mounting board to protect the artwork.'

'Order whatever you need,' he said.

'Thanks. It means that you can actually look at the artwork without touching it—the oils on your fingertips can do damage, plus graphite, chalk and pastels are very easily smudged.'

'I'm learning more about art than I ever thought I'd need,' he said wryly.

She flinched. 'Sorry. I don't mean to be boring.'

'You're not. My work's in a very different area and Nonno always calls me a philistine,' Angelo said.

'I did notice that you don't seem to have any artwork on your walls,' she said before she could stop herself.

'I don't really have any opinions on art.'

'Noted, and I'll shut up.'

'You could teach me.' Then he looked shocked, as if he hadn't expected to say that.

Was this an area where maybe they could connect?

Part of her thought she should back off and

leave it. But part of her couldn't resist. 'If you came to meet Jeremy, my tutor, tomorrow,' she said tentatively, 'then maybe we can go to a gallery round the corner afterwards. We can look at a couple of paintings and see what you like or don't like—just style and composition, nothing too heavy.'

'All right,' he said.

This wasn't a date.

It was about helping him understand art and maybe understanding his grandfather more.

Everything was fine until the middle of the afternoon, when Mariana was making coffee. She'd taken off her shoes while she'd photographed a couple of sketches, and had padded into the kitchen barefoot. She'd mistimed using the frother so the milk bubbled over, scalding her hands; as she dropped the metal jug, she accidentally knocked one of the mugs off the worktop, and it smashed on the slate floor.

Angelo was there in what felt like a nanosecond. 'Stand still!' he barked.

She thought of when she'd dropped things in her own kitchen and Eric had been furious; it made her freeze.

To her shock, Angelo walked over to her, lifted her up, and carried her over to the chairs at the far end of the kitchen. Gently, he set her down on her feet again. 'Stay there,' he said, 'and I'll clear this up so you don't cut your foot on a shard.'

'I'm sorry,' she whispered. 'I...'

Then he noticed her hand. 'Wait,' he said, grabbed a tea towel from a drawer and tipped ice into it from the freezer. 'OK. Keep that over the burn until I've cleared this up and then you can put your hand under cold running water,' he directed.

Once he'd cleared up, he looked at her. 'Where are your shoes?'

'With Leo's boxes.'

'I'll get them.' He fetched her shoes, then waited until she put them on. 'Are you all right? Let me look at your hand.'

To her horror, she burst into tears.

Something was clearly very wrong—something more than just a simple scald. Angelo didn't have a clue what to do. Would she take it the wrong way if he wrapped his arms around her and held her to comfort her? On the other hand, he couldn't just ignore her distress.

In the end, he decided to treat her as if she was his sister. He wrapped his arms around her and held her until she stopped crying.

'Sorry. I didn't mean to have a meltdown on you.' She wiped her eyes with the back of her hand. 'I'll pay for the mug I broke.'

'It's fine. Accidents happen. But I get the feeling that there's more to it than—' he grimaced '—literally spilt milk. Do you need me to take you to hospital?'

'Hospital?'

'The burn on your hand,' he reminded her.

She shook her head. 'You gave me ice to cool the skin. It'll be fine. It's more shock than anything else.'

That looked like a lot more than shock to him.

He must've spoken aloud, because she said, 'I'm sorry. I owe you an explanation.' She took a deep breath. 'My ex got a bit angry if I broke something.'

'He *hit* you?' Angelo looked at her in disbelief.

'No. It was never physical.' She looked away. 'He was a control freak. He liked everything in its right place.'

Which was pretty much what Angelo had said to her about himself.

Had she worn a business suit and high heels today because he thought he expected it of her? he wondered.

'He used to tell me how useless I was. He brought up every single mistake I'd ever made, any time I did anything wrong. To the point where I realised how useless and stupid I was, and I was lucky he even bothered with me.'

'Nobody has the right to treat another human being like that,' Angelo said. 'I read that interview you gave, but I didn't realise how badly it had affected you.'

'I'm getting there,' she said. 'That's why I studied so hard, to prove to myself that I'm more than Eric made me think I was.'

'You *are*,' he said.

'I know. But every so often something knocks me a bit. I'm sorry.'

'Don't apologise. You've done nothing wrong,' he said.

She bit her lip. 'I understand if you want me to leave right now. You have to protect your grandfather.'

'I don't want you to leave,' he said. 'I knew a little bit of what happened before I asked you to help. Do you have an injunction in place?'

'Yes.' She lifted her chin. 'He breached it once, and because of that he has a suspended sentence. He won't risk getting put in prison.'

'Then there's nothing to worry about,' Angelo said. 'I'd very much like you to carry on with the excellent job you're doing of sorting out my grandfather's papers and prove that that painting is what he thinks it is. You're the one person I believe has the knowledge and skills to make it happen. But I'm also going to drive you home tonight, and I'll pick you up tomorrow morning.'

'That's the point, Angelo,' she said. 'If I spend the rest of my life looking over my shoulder, worrying about if Eric will get to me, then he wins. I want to live my life *well*. To be as independent as possible.'

He thought about it.

Then he thought about it some more.

'I want,' Angelo said, 'to give you another hug. Except I don't want you to take it the wrong way. I'm just thinking this sort of thing could've happened to my sister, or my colleagues, or people I know. And it's horrifying.'

'A hug,' she said, 'would be nice.'

He held her close. 'And I'm sorry if I've made you feel that I'm a control freak.'

'You kind of are. But I know you're looking out for your grandfather. It's not quite the same thing.'

'I hope not,' he said. 'I'm going to make you a coffee. And you're going to promise to tell me if you're in the slightest bit worried.'

When he was holding her like this, cherishing her and protecting her, Mariana couldn't have felt any less worried. 'Thank you,' she said.

She settled down to work again. An hour or so later, Angelo said, 'I've got it! Look at this.' He came over to her desk and placed the diary in front of her.

Leo's handwriting was hard to read, and everything was in Italian. She squinted at the pages.

As if guessing what the problem was, Angelo said, 'I've been working on this for a while so I'm used to Nonno's handwriting. You'd expect an ex–art student to have that lovely spiky handwriting, but this is an atrocious scrawl. Shall I translate?'

'I've got as far as the word "April",' she said with a smile, 'so it might be a fair bit quicker if you do it.'

He smiled back. 'My grandfather planned to visit a village called Barrington in Norfolk, where he knew Carulli had spent a couple of summers painting. He wanted to see if the cottage where Carulli had stayed was still there. He flew to London, then took the train to Norwich.' He leafed through a few pages. 'It's the middle of May 1963. Here, he says he looked around the antique shops in Norwich. He bought some sketches and two watercolours, then took the train to Holt—the town nearest to Barrington. Apparently it was full of antique shops and bookshops, and he found some Carulli sketches there, too.'

He turned over to another page. 'He walked from Holt to Barrington because that was the only way to get to the village. He found the cottages, took photographs and talked to the people who lived there. They worked on the farm belonging to the big house, and so had their family as far back as they remembered, but there weren't any family stories about the Italian painter who'd come to stay in the village nearly a hundred years ago. He stayed in the Red Lion—the village pub—and he went up to the farmhouse to see if they knew anything.'

'Did they?'

'No. They suggested trying the big house.'

'And that's where he found the painting?'

Angelo grinned. 'Yes.'

'That's brilliant!' She flung her arms around him.

And then she remembered where she was, and pulled back. 'Sorry. I got a bit overexcited because we've solved another bit of the puzzle.' She didn't dare quite meet his eyes. Or admit to herself that holding him in her arms, even briefly, had stirred up all kinds of odd feelings. Her relationship with Angelo Beresford had to remain strictly business. They wanted different things out of life. They weren't compatible. She couldn't trust the attraction.

'He was lucky the painting wasn't lost for ever,' Angelo said. 'They were renovating the house and had just cleared out the attic—they'd actually thrown the painting in a skip because it had been eaten by mice in one corner and they thought it was worthless. He asked if he could see it anyway and they said he could have it. My grandfather recognised what it was—the farmhouse he'd seen earlier, which had barely changed since Carulli painted it— and insisted on giving them money for it. He photographed the big house and the painting, as well as the farmhouse, and then he took the painting back to Italy and had a friend restore it in Florence.'

'What a story,' Mariana said. 'That bit alone makes *The Girl in the Window* a really good candidate for the show.'

'So is there a biography somewhere that says where Carulli painted things and when, to help us tie down the date?' Angelo asked.

She nodded. 'We know he went to England in the eighteen-sixties. He toured East Anglia and there are some watercolours—harvest scenes with trees, haystacks, poppies—but no oils. There's a possibility that the one with the poppies might have been an early study for *The Girl in the Window*. I'd need to check.' She bit her lip. 'But if the people at the house were going to give the painting to Leo for nothing and he insisted on giving them money, that suggests to me that there isn't going to be an invoice or a receipt.'

'Would he have asked them for a letter or something?' Angelo asked. 'Given that he was a collector and he would've known the importance of provenance?'

'Maybe,' she said. 'But if he was so thrilled about finding the painting and so shocked that it had almost been thrown out and lost for ever, he might not have been thinking clearly enough to ask at the time.'

'And if there's no paper evidence...'

'Then we have to build the case,' she said. 'I'm guessing there would be an invoice and a note from the restorer stating exactly what he'd done.' She flicked into her computer file.

'What your grandfather says in the diary tallies exactly with what he told us.'

'Hopefully he'll have a receipt from his stay at the village pub. And he said he took photographs. We need to find them, and whether the pub is still there, and if anyone remembers my grandfather,' Angelo said.

'There might be a local history society who can suggest leads if we get stuck,' Mariana said.

'You're right. I'll go online and see what I can find out,' Angelo said.

'I'll make a start on the boxes while you check out the pub,' she said. 'I'll put any artwork to one side, and just sort the rest into one pile a year for now.'

'Good idea.'

Half an hour later, he came down to join her. 'There's a local history group. According to their website, the pub closed in the nineteen-eighties and was turned into a private house. There's no phone number so I've emailed to ask what they can tell us.' He frowned. 'All we can do now is wait.'

She had a feeling that waiting wasn't something that came easily to him. 'Then let's concentrate on this. I've made a start on the piles.'

He worked methodically—as she'd expected—and on a couple of occasions their hands brushed together when they reached across the table at the same time. She was so aware of him. Of his strength—he'd lifted her so easily in the kitchen—and of his gentleness. The way he was letting her run the project her way rather than micromanaging it himself.

But most of all she thought about how it had felt when he'd held her. He'd been sensitive. How would it feel if he held her with passion?

She glanced at him—only to find he was giving her the same kind of sidelong glance. Did he feel the same pull of attraction that she did? Did he, too, wonder what would happen if they took a risk? Her mouth went dry as the possibilities slid through her mind.

But when he made no move, she made herself concentrate on the task in hand.

The afternoon netted them absolutely nothing from May 1963.

'This is starting to feel like looking for a needle in a haystack,' Angelo said.

'That's because we're in the early stages. It'll come together,' she said, slightly more confidently than she felt.

'I guess. I'd really like to find some photos, though.'

'We'll get there,' she said. 'Let's do another hour.'

He looked at his watch. 'I can't expect you to work the same stupid hours as I would.'

'You're going to carry on if I leave, aren't you?' she asked.

'Well—yes,' he admitted.

'Then I'll stay,' she said. 'I want to be here when we find the evidence.'

And it was a sense of diligence in her work that drove her, she told herself. Nothing to do with spending more time with Angelo.

He looked at the unopened boxes. 'We're not going to get it all done today.'

'No, but we'll get quite a bit done in an hour,' she said.

'OK. On condition I buy you dinner.'

Dinner. Just the two of them. Much more intimate than lunch at his kitchen table. She almost suggested that they go out—but he was her client. She couldn't afford complications. Instead, she said, 'A takeaway. Delivered here. And we go halves.'

'Deal.'

Another hour of searching, and it still felt as if they'd barely scratched the surface. Although they'd found some photos, the pictures weren't from 1963 and they weren't taken in England.

'That looks like the arches by the Uffizi, just before you get to the Ponte Vecchio,' Angelo said. 'That's definitely my great-grandfather and my mother. Cammie really looked like her at that age.' He took a snap of the photographs with his phone. 'I'm going to send this to them both now, because they'll enjoy this. Mamma might remember something about this—she looks as if she was about ten at the time.'

'From the way he's looking at her, clearly your great-grandfather adored her,' Mariana said. 'That's such a lovely photo.'

'I found some reels of cine film while I was packing the boxes,' he said. 'They're from the nineteen-fifties so they're nothing to do with Nonno's visit to Norfolk, but I'm getting them transferred to a digital format because I think they're from when my grandparents were first married and from when my mother was small, and I think she and Nonno would enjoy seeing them.'

'Like my sister and me asking my parents to play the videos they took when we were little,' Mariana said. 'It's lovely to have those memories.' She'd thought to have similar films of her own child by now. Until everything had gone wrong. 'I have lots of clips of Olly on my phone. He pinches Sophie's phone, records himself telling a terrible joke and sends it to me—and half the time he's laughing so much that he can hardly tell me the punchline.'

Again, there was fleeting sadness in Angelo's eyes. Regret for the children he could have had? But he'd told her he didn't want children and that was why his marriage had ended. Or maybe she'd misread his expression and he was bored.

Thankfully the pizza arrived and saved her from another faux pas.

A few minutes later, Angelo's phone pinged. 'That's a text from my mother,' he said, glancing at the screen. 'I'll check what she wants later.'

'It might be your grandfather,' she said.

'No. She would've called.'

Unless she couldn't.

She could see from his expression that he'd just thought of the same thing.

'Check it,' she said gently. 'You're not being rude.'

He nodded in acknowledgement and opened the message. 'It's not *Nonno*.'

'Good.' But she could still see the fear in his eyes. She had to work faster. Make this happen for Angelo, before it was too late.

'She loved the photo. Apparently it was taken after one of my mother's Tuesday singing lessons. Her teacher lived on the other side of the Ponte Vecchio,' he said. 'And she's thrilled to have it.'

'That's good. Fingers crossed we'll find the photos we want tomorrow,' Mariana said. 'Get our breakthrough.' And it was the excitement of the chase that she was looking forward to, she told herself. Being close to Angelo had nothing to do with it.

* * *

'I'll drive you home,' Angelo said when they'd finished the pizza.

'On condition we do another half an hour on the boxes first,' Mariana said.

He couldn't help smiling. 'Everyone in my office says I'm a workaholic. But you're just as bad, aren't you?'

'I love this kind of work,' she said.

'OK. As long as you don't feel I'm bullying you into working stupid hours.'

'You're not bullying me. I know the difference,' she said quietly.

Her ex. Of course. He winced. 'Sorry. I didn't mean to bring up difficult memories for you.'

'It's fine.' She paused. 'Are you still OK to meet my tutor tomorrow morning?'

'Sure.'

'And then we'll have half an hour in the National afterwards,' she said, 'which is just round the corner, and I'll work late tomorrow to make up the time.'

'Strictly speaking, you're my consultant rather than my employee, and you're not on an hourly rate. You set your own working hours,' he reminded her.

'I know, but…' She spread her hands. 'I want to get this bit done.'

'Is it worth me hiring a temp to help us?' he asked.

She shook her head. 'If there are too many people working on something, things can get misfiled or missed.'

'You want to be the one who finds the evidence, don't you?'

'Yes. You or me,' she said. 'We're a team.'

His heart missed a beat.

A team.

Then he reminded himself that she was talking about work. Not personal stuff. Given her past, she'd no doubt be wary in the extreme of getting involved with anyone again. And he didn't exactly come without complications. He needed to bury his attraction towards her— just like he'd buried his emotions ever since his divorce. Cool, calm and collected. That was him. He'd focus on the excitement of the search and not on how much he was enjoying spending time with her and getting to know her.

He drove her home, and agreed to meet her at the university entrance in the morning.

And then he went home to work on the journals. At least they had their first bit of evidence; he photocopied the relevant pages, marked them with a sticky note, and typed up and printed a translation.

Tomorrow, perhaps, they'd find another piece of the puzzle.

CHAPTER SIX

ON WEDNESDAY MORNING, Angelo met Mariana at the university. She was leaning against the wall, reading a book, as he arrived; today she was back to wearing jeans, canvas shoes and a T-shirt, with her hair caught back in a scarf. She looked much more relaxed than she had the previous day, he thought, and he felt slightly out of place in his suit. But a dull corporate lawyer was exactly what he'd been ever since his divorce, working to fill his life and not let himself feel anything.

Oh, honestly. His life was fine just as it was. He didn't need anything else.

'Good morning,' he said as he reached her. And her smile was so sweet that it actually made his heart miss a beat.

'Hi.' She slipped the book into her bag. 'Come and meet Jeremy.'

He reined himself in and followed her to her tutor's office. The room was almost as untidy as his grandfather's office, with books in chaotic piles everywhere and pictures and articles torn from magazines pinned haphazardly to a cork board. Had it not been for what he'd seen of Mariana's neat working habits, Angelo would've thought that the old cliché about being artistic and disorganised was actually true.

'Very pleased to meet you, Mr Beresford.' Jeremy Hartley shook his hand warmly.

'Angelo, please. And you, Dr Hartley,' Angelo replied politely.

'Jeremy. Mariana's shown me photographs of your grandfather's collection—and it's incredible.'

'I did have a bit of a moment when I walked into the *palazzo* and saw the paintings—just like Carter must've felt when he realised he'd found Tutankhamun's tomb,' Mariana confessed with a smile. 'And it's a real privilege to help catalogue them.'

'Knowing about all these new paintings is going to change things we thought we knew about Carulli,' Jeremy said. 'I know it's a bit forward of me to ask, Angelo, but if there's any chance I could visit your grandfather and see the paintings, I would be so grateful.'

'He's not in the best of health,' Angelo said. 'But knowing that you're interested in his collection and that you believe his unsigned painting is a Carulli—that might help to brighten him a little, so I'm happy to arrange a visit.'

'Thank you. Obviously I wouldn't stay long or do anything to tire him out,' Jeremy said. 'I'll be guided totally by you.'

'I've been going through Carulli's biography,' Mariana said, taking the book she'd been reading earlier out of her bag. 'He stayed in England in 1862 and 1863 in a little Norfolk village called Barrington—which is where Leo found the painting, a century later. Leo's journal mentions buying sketches, and I found a preliminary sketch the other day for his painting *Tuscan Harvest*—it's signed and dated and he made a note about the location on the back. I'm hoping that he's done something similar with our painting so we can prove it stayed where he painted it.' She grimaced. 'Sorry, Angelo. I mean your grandfather's painting.'

'You love it as much as he does. I don't think he'd mind you calling it "ours",' he said, smiling at her. Did she have any idea how cute she was when she was all fired up and enthusiastic? She glowed with happiness, and it made him feel warm inside.

'So do you have any provenance for the painting yet?' Jeremy asked.

'I'm building the case,' Mariana said. 'But I want to send it for X-rays to see if there are any underlying sketches, and we need to check if the pigment is the same as that in his other English paintings.'

'Good idea,' Jeremy said. 'Do the composition and brushstrokes match his usual style?'

'Yes.' She filled Jeremy in on their work so far.

'It's the kind of thing all scholars dream about finding,' Jeremy said, 'or at least being part of the discovery. An unknown, unsigned Carulli, and others from the same era we've not known about before. How utterly amazing.'

'I'll speak to my grandfather and arrange a

visit,' Angelo said. 'And I assume you need some time to discuss whatever you usually discuss with Mariana.'

'In the circumstances,' Jeremy said, 'that's your call, Mariana.'

'I'd rather like to go back to working on our research and seeing what it uncovers, because it's going to affect my thesis,' Mariana said. 'But I'll keep you updated, Jeremy.'

'And I'll be in touch to discuss your visit to my grandfather,' Angelo said. 'Actually, I'm going to Florence on Saturday, if you're free.'

'Saturday? Let me see if I can move a couple of things around,' Jeremy said, 'and I'll let you know.'

When they left her tutor's office, Mariana looked at Angelo. 'We agreed, thirty minutes in the National.'

'All right,' he said.

'Let's start with something older.' She led him through the rooms. 'Botticelli,' she said. 'Late fifteenth century. This isn't quite as famous as his paintings in the Uffizi, but this is *Venus and Mars*. It shows Venus awake and Mars asleep—in other words, love conquers war.' She grinned. 'And then you've got the rude bits.'

'Rude bits? But they're fully clothed,' Angelo said, frowning.

'Take a closer look. The little satyrs have pinched his lance and, even though one of them is blowing a trumpet in his ear, Mars isn't waking up. He's…um…*unarmed*,' she said.

Angelo suddenly realised what she meant.

'You mean they've just had sex and he's gone to sleep?' He felt hot all over. How on earth had he ended up discussing sex with Mariana Thackeray in the middle of a public art gallery?

The warmth must've shown in his face, because she gave him the cheekiest grin. One that made his heart skip a beat. One that made him want to kiss her and see if he could rouse corresponding heat in her. Even though he knew it was a bad idea, it was hard to resist. How soft would her mouth be against his? How would it feel to have her arms wrapped round him in passion?

'There's always something to spot in a painting,' she said. 'Do you like it?'

'It's pretty enough,' he said, trying to be diplomatic.

'But you wouldn't want it on your walls.'

'I wouldn't spend time gazing at it, no,' he admitted.

'So it doesn't move you.'

'No.' *She* moved him. The fact that right now he could do with a cold shower had nothing to do with the painting and everything to do with her.

'OK. Renaissance paintings might not be your thing—even though half your family comes from Florence.' She took him into another room. 'How about this? Constable's *The Hay Wain.*'

'It's a pretty landscape,' he said, again trying to be diplomatic and hoping she wasn't going to start waxing lyrical over the shape of the clouds. As far as he was concerned, it was just a picture—something he'd glance at but wouldn't snag his attention.

'The area still looks like that today,' she said. 'But I can see from your face that you're being polite. Early nineteenth-century landscape isn't your thing, either. How about a seascape?' She took him around the corner. 'Turner's *The Fighting Temeraire*.'

Now this one he liked a bit more. And he knew she'd press him for details. 'I like the sky,' he said.

'But not the ship?'

He wrinkled his nose.

'OK. We can work with sky. Let's try something from a bit later in the century.' She took him into another room. 'This is Monet's *Flood Waters*.'

He shook his head. 'Not this one. It's a bit…' He paused to find the right word. 'Wishy-washy.'

She grinned. 'That's one way to describe water. Perhaps not French Impressionism, then.' She led him around the corner. 'How about this one?'

'Even I can recognise van Gogh,' he said. 'The *Sunflowers*.'

'How does it make you feel?' she asked.

'It's like sunshine,' he said. 'It's bright. I like this one.'

'Happiness,' she said. 'Good. So we've established that you like happy paintings and sunshine.'

'Or that I'm just dull and like the popular stuff.'

'There's nothing wrong with liking popular stuff,' she said. 'And you're not dull.' She looked thoughtful. 'I know I said not French Impressionism, but it's the light and shade that your grandfather really loves in the Macchiaioli paintings. Me, too. I'm going to show you something else.' She led him round the corner. 'This one is pastels rather than oil. It's Degas, *After the Bath.*'

The seated woman's naked back and upper thigh were visible, the curve of her waist to the right, and her arms. 'It's all about movement, the blurred contours,' she said.

Angelo thought of Mariana. How she would look, seated in the same pose. The softness and warmth of her skin, the bright gleam of her hair… And his mouth went dry. He could almost smell the floral scent she wore, the dampness of her skin, imagine how she'd drop that towel and turn to look at him over her shoulder, her lips parted.

'*Now* you look as if you get it,' she whispered in his ear. 'How art can move you. Make you think. Make you *feel*.'

He almost—*almost*—wrapped his arms around her and kissed her right there and then, in the middle of the gallery, heedless of the fact that it was a very public place.

But he held himself back. Just.

'I get it,' he said, hearing the crack in his own voice.

'Good. Enough art for now,' she said. 'But another time I'm going to take you to see the Degas dancers at the Courtauld. I think you'll like them. Turner's skies, Degas's figures and the brightness of van Gogh. I'll have a think about what else you might enjoy.'

They spent the rest of the morning working through the boxes, but Angelo couldn't shake his awareness of Mariana. Several times he glanced up from the papers to see her glancing at him, too, and looking away as if she felt guilty about being caught.

So did she feel the same weird pull of attraction towards him—even though they both knew this wasn't sensible?

And what were they going to do about it?

He kept himself under strict control for the rest of the morning—until he came across a card envelope. 'Ferrania Color,' he said.

Mariana frowned. 'What's that?'

'The Italian version of Kodak,' he said. 'Mamma has some envelopes like these. Italian-developed photographs from when she was young.'

Mariana's eyes widened. 'Do you think this might be...?'

'The photographs from Nonno's visit to Norfolk? Hold your breath and wish.' Which was exactly what he did as he drew the photographs out of their envelope.

The photographs were square, with a narrow white border, showing that they were older than modern prints; they were glossy, and most importantly they were in colour.

He felt sick with nerves. 'I really think this might be it.'

The first couple of pictures were of a row of flint cottages, with red tiled roofs and a decorative border of bricks around the white-painted windows and door. The front garden was full of summer flowers.

'Look on the back,' she whispered. 'Just in case he wrote something.'

He turned it over and his grandfather's handwriting was obvious. *"'New Road Cottages. 1963. Carulli stayed here,'"* he translated.

'Oh, my God,' she said. 'He's tracked down the actual cottages.'

The next photograph was of another building with a steep red tiled roof and small windows; it looked as if it, too, was made from brick and flint, but the entire building had been painted white. There was a tiny porch over the front door, and on the front of the building was a large black sign with 'Red Lion' and a stylised lion painted on it in red.

'We're getting closer. This was where Nonno said he stayed in the village,' Angelo said.

There were two more photographs of the pub, and then one of a large house.

'Do you think that's the "big house" he talked about?' she asked.

'But it's not the house that's actually in his painting,' Angelo said.

Mariana checked her notes. 'He went to the farmhouse, and they suggested trying the big house. So maybe this is the farmhouse.'

Angelo turned to the next photograph. 'No. This one looks like the farmhouse in the painting.'

'Agreed,' she said.

When he flipped over to the next photograph, he dropped the lot on the table. 'It's Nonno. Outside the big house. With the painting showing the farmhouse. And you can see where the canvas wasn't framed, where the mice ate the corner,' he whispered.

'It all ties in with everything he told us,' Mariana said, putting her arms around him and hugging him. 'We've found it. And this is bona fide documentary evidence that no expert would ignore or say is just circumstantial.'

The next thing he knew, his mouth was against hers and he was kissing her. Really kissing her. And she was kissing him back, her lips warm and sweet, giving and demanding at the same time.

The world spun on its axis.

He shouldn't be doing this. She was vulnerable, she'd been hurt, and if her biological clock started ticking then he'd end up letting her down. She was off limits.

And if he let himself fall for her and the whole thing went wrong, the same way it had gone wrong with Stephanie, he'd end up with his heart broken a second time. Better not to risk it in the first place. He needed to stop this. Right now.

With an effort, he tore his mouth from hers. 'I'm sorry. I shouldn't have… That was unprofessional, and I apologise.'

She took a step back from him. 'It wasn't just you. We both got carried away with the excitement of finding the photographs.'

It was an excuse, and he knew it. But he took it gratefully. 'Yes.'

'We'll pretend it didn't happen,' she said.

'Good idea.' He took a breath. 'I'll go and make us coffee.'

'I'll keep going with the paperwork,' she said.

Putting distance between them would definitely help, he thought, and left the room before he said something foolish. Or before he did something reckless like hauling her back into his arms and kissing her until they were both senseless.

Mariana closed her eyes when Angelo had left the room. How could she have been so stupid?

Eric's voice echoed in her head.

Who on earth do you think would be interested in you?

The contempt. The sneer in his voice.

She shook herself. No. She'd moved on. And she would find someone else to share her life with. Just... Maybe not yet.

By the time Angelo came back with coffee, she'd unearthed a couple more important pieces of paper.

'I've found the receipts for the sketches your grandfather bought in Norwich,' she said.

He read it out loud. '*"Study of a farmhouse, pencil on paper, signed and inscribed, Domenico Carulli. Nine inches by twelve inches."* Hopefully that's our farmhouse.' He blinked.

'And he paid twenty-five pounds for a sketch, back in 1963? That's a lot of money.'

'Your grandfather had a good eye,' she said.

He looked at the second receipt. '"*Study of a female, pencil on paper, signed. Twelve inches by nine inches. Domenico Carulli. Inscription on reverse: Alice.*" Do you think that was the model's name?'

'Possibly. Or he might have written it on the back of the paper for another reason. Given the size, they sound as if they came from a sketch-book,' she said. 'If the dealer is still around, we can ask to see the records, or they might be in an archive. We can check where the dealer bought the sketches, and trace them back.'

'That's good.'

She noticed that he didn't meet her gaze and he was gripping his mug of coffee. Was he, too, thinking about that kiss? She was trying really hard to put it out of her head and pretend it hadn't happened, just as they'd agreed, but she couldn't help thinking about it. How soft and sweet and promising that kiss had been. How much she wanted to do it again. Angelo Beresford was one of the good guys as well as being the most gorgeous man she'd ever met. And yet there was a reserve in him. She knew he was divorced and he'd sidestepped any attempt to discuss his private life.

This whole thing was so new and so unexpected. She needed time to get used to the idea. To work out if she could trust her judgement this time, or if she was heading for trouble again. So it would be best to keep everything on a strictly work footing for now.

'Paperwork,' she said, and carefully set her mug down on the floor. At his raised eyebrow, she explained, 'Given my habit of knocking things over, this is safest.'

'I hope you're not still worrying about that.'

'No,' she fibbed.

'But I get your point. If we spill anything on these papers, it could be disastrous.' He put his own mug on the floor. 'Let's keep going. I assume we're looking out for those two sketches as well?'

'And the watercolours, because they might be studies for the painting.'

They kept going.

'Here we go,' she said, a while later. 'A study

of a woman, about the right size, and the word "Alice" is written on the back. And he's signed it.'

'Is she the girl in the painting?' he asked.

She went over to one of the files and took out a print of the photograph. 'What do you think?'

'I can't really tell,' he said. 'It's too small.'

'Let's look at the photograph on my computer. We can zoom in,' she said.

They took the sketch up to Angelo's office and she opened the photograph on her laptop; Angelo stood next to her, so close that she could feel the warmth of his body. She still couldn't get that kiss out of her head. What would happen if she looked up at him and tipped her head back, inviting another kiss? Would he kiss her? Or would he back away?

She just about managed to get a grip on her emotions and zoomed in to the model's face.

'It's her,' they said at the same time.

'So if this model is Alice...'

'It still doesn't prove she lived in the farmhouse,' she said. 'My guess is he'd been thinking about the composition for a while and sketched different elements. And I'm really hoping for a date on that farmhouse sketch so we can say it ties in to the painting.'

'It needs to be 1862 or 1863,' he said.

She nodded. 'And we need other evidence to prove that the model's name was Alice. Have you heard anything back from the local history society?'

'Not yet,' he said.

'OK. Let's keep going.'

They went back to the papers, and found the farmhouse sketch next.

'There's a date on the back. 1862,' Angelo said.

'So we have more evidence that fits together: the model and the farmhouse, both signed and one dated,' she said. 'I need to call Nigel.'

Nigel was delighted by the news. 'I need to come and see them for myself.'

She put her phone into speaker mode. 'Angelo, Nigel wants to come and see what we have. It's your call. Do you want to take the evidence to the studio or for Nigel to come to us?'

'I'd prefer Nigel to come to us, if that's OK with him, because I don't want to stop looking. I want to see if there's more about Alice in these boxes,' he said.

'I'm in meetings for the rest of today. Can I call in tonight on the way home from the studio?' Nigel asked.

'Sure,' Angelo said, and gave him the address. When Mariana ended the call, he looked at her. 'Isn't Wednesday the evening you usually spend with your nephew?'

'Yes.' She bit her lip. 'If I stay for the meeting with Nigel, I'll have to swap nights. I'll text my sister to let her know I can't make it.'

'Family's important,' Angelo said.

'I know.' Wasn't that the whole reason he'd asked her to help? Because his grandfather was important to him? 'But so is this project.'

'Then we'll ask Nigel to make it another evening,' he suggested.

She sighed. 'There are days when I really wish I could be in two places at once. I'll text Sophie to see if she can switch her date night to tomorrow, and I'll promise Olly a new book. We've just discovered this series about Roman children who solve mysteries and I loved reading to him.'

'Sounds good.'

Though was it her imagination or was there a tiny hint of longing and despair in his expression? She blinked, and it was gone. Then again, he'd said his marriage broke up because he didn't want children, so it must've been her imagination.

She texted Sophie, who replied instantly that it was fine. 'I'm going tomorrow instead,' she said with a smile. And she almost, *almost* asked him if he'd like to come with her. But of course he wouldn't. He had his own work to catch up on. And, although he had a new niece, he barely talked about her. He obviously wasn't that keen on children.

Although they managed to sort out a lot of the papers, they found nothing else from the period they both really wanted to know about by the time that Nigel arrived.

'Good to meet you, Mr Beresford,' Nigel said.

'Angelo,' Angelo said, shaking his hand.

Nigel looked at the evidence they'd found. 'There's not quite enough, yet,' he said. 'Your main painting could be by another artist.'

'Someone who studied with him,' Mariana agreed. 'Except his biographer didn't turn up any evidence.'

'Or maybe his biographer didn't realise it was important,' Nigel said. 'If you're wading through letters and diaries to tell someone's life, how do you decide what to use and what to leave out?'

'The letters are in Florence,' she said. 'We could check those.'

'Find the evidence and we'll get a camera out there,' Nigel said. 'I just want one more link in the chain before I give this the go-ahead.'

'Whether you film it or not,' Angelo said, 'we're doing the research. Is the archive in Florence open on Saturday?'

Mariana checked on her phone. 'No. Monday to Friday, by appointment.'

'Save their number. I'll call them first thing tomorrow and make an appointment,' Angelo said.

CHAPTER SEVEN

ON THURSDAY MORNING, Angelo rang the archive in Florence. Mariana could hear him speaking in fluent Italian while she worked through the next layer of papers. Then he moved the phone away from his ear and turned to her. 'They can fit us in tomorrow. Does that work for you?'

'Of course.'

'Good.' He smiled at her—a smile that gave her goosebumps—and resumed his conversation. 'They're going to have the papers ready for us tomorrow,' he said when he'd ended the call. 'I'll book our flight for first thing in the morning.'

'Great. Thanks.'

As they continued working on the papers, Mariana found herself glancing at him, remembering that kiss. *Kisses*—because it had happened more than once.

Could she trust her judgement, this time round?

And, if she could, would it be better to wait until after they'd finished this project? It was a complication she thought both of them could do without. Yet, at the same time, she was so drawn to him. He was the first man since Eric who'd made her want to take an emotional risk.

A couple of times their hands accidentally touched while they were sorting out the papers, and it made her skin tingle where his fingers touched hers. Was it the same for him? She dared not look at him, just in case she was making a fool of herself.

'Do you want to leave earlier tonight?' Angelo asked. 'You've put in a lot of hours this week, and I'm guessing you want to spend some time with your nephew before he goes to bed.'

She wasn't quite sure whether Angelo wanted to put some space between them, or if he was genuinely being kind. Maybe both. 'Thanks,' she said.

* * *

She was still none the wiser when she got to her sister's house.

'I want to know everything,' Sophie warned her with a smile.

Mariana filled her in on the situation while she helped Olly build a train track.

'It all sounds right up your street—and how exciting, solving a mystery about your favourite painter,' Sophie said. 'Though there's something you're not telling me.'

Mariana sighed. 'Angelo.'

'Problem?'

Mariana wrinkled her nose. 'He's nice. It's not a problem about work.'

Sophie looked at her. 'Do you like him?'

Mariana nodded.

'That's good. And you need a nice guy, after what Eric put you through.'

'It's complicated,' Mariana said.

'He doesn't feel the same?'

'We haven't discussed it—but I think he does.'

'What's the problem, then?' Sophie frowned.

'Please tell me you're not going to let Eric get in the way.'

'No. Angelo knows what happened.'

'Then what?'

'He's divorced.' She paused. 'His ex wanted children.'

'And he doesn't?' Sophie winced. 'So he doesn't want the same things that you do from life. And having children is one of the really big ones—there isn't a halfway house.'

'Plus he's my client. I need to be professional.'

'Maybe,' Sophie said, 'you just need to get it out of your system.'

'I don't think either of us is the mad fling type.'

'Maybe you should be,' Sophie said. 'Think about it. And you're going to Florence with him again this weekend.'

'And we're staying in his grandfather's house,' Mariana pointed out. 'So, no. A fling is out of the question.'

'You should talk about it, though.'

Mariana shook her head. 'Better to leave things as they are. No awkwardness.'

'Just silent smoulders between you? That,' Sophie said, 'is asking for trouble.'

'Less trouble than getting everything wrong.'

Sophie hugged her. 'Mariana, you're gorgeous and you're lovely and you're bright. You just need to trust yourself.'

'I got it wrong last time.'

'Which doesn't mean you make the same mistakes again.' Sophie paused. 'I know how to fix this. Invite him for dinner. Mum and I will vet him.'

Mariana looked at her sister in horror. 'Absolutely not!'

'The offer is there,' Sophie said, completely unrepentant. 'Trust yourself, or let us vet him.'

'It's fine,' Mariana said. 'We're working together.'

'Then get to know him. Really know him. And when the project is over, if you still like him, then proposition him. You have nothing to lose,' Sophie advised.

'Maybe,' Mariana said, and changed the subject to the new book she'd bought at lunchtime for Olly. Her sister's smile said she knew what Mariana was doing and would let her off— for now.

The next morning, Angelo picked Mariana up in the taxi on the way to the airport; he liked the fact that she was already waiting outside for him, ready to go.

Professional.

Just as he needed her to be. Because it really wasn't fair to dump his past on her. He knew she wanted something from life that he couldn't give her. So this whole thing about his heart skipping a beat every time she smiled at him had to stop.

To hammer the point home, he asked, 'How was your nephew?'

She smiled. 'We had a good time playing trains—and he loved the new story. Sophie is going to read a chapter a night, and I promised him we'll finish the book next week.'

He could see the delight she took in her nephew; and it underlined for him what a fabulous mother she would make. How could he deny her that opportunity? It wouldn't be fair.

Once he'd got his head back in control of his heart, he changed the subject to Carulli and enjoyed her passion for the painter all the way to Florence.

At the train station, they took a taxi straight to the archives. As promised, Carulli's letters were ready for them, and Mariana had produced a working file for them to scribble on with a timeline of what she knew from his biography, notes of Leo's memories, the translation from the journals and prints of the painting and sketches.

They put their baggage in one of the lockers, though Mariana kept her laptop and camera out, and settled themselves in a corner of the reading room with the letters. 'I'll read them out in English, and you stop me if you think it's important,' he said.

'OK. That's tricky handwriting,' she said, leaning over his shoulder. 'I'm glad you're here, because it would take me a while to work out what the words are, let alone translating.'

She was glad he was here...

For business purposes, he reminded himself. To be her translator because he was bilingual, having an English father and an Italian mother.

The letters to Carulli's brother from 1862 told them that Domenico had met several other painters in London, had visited Norwich and Holt, and then gone to Barrington.

'But he doesn't say where he's staying, just that the harvest scenes are delightfully rustic,' Angelo said, frustrated. He raked his hand through his hair. 'There's no mention of Alice.'

'Her name might not even be Alice,' she reminded him. 'It could've been just a note to himself about someone completely different. Unless we find definitive evidence linking a name with the painting, we can't make any assumptions.'

'OK. Let's carry on.'

They followed Carulli back to Florence, and then back to England again the following spring. 'He says something here about being a drawing master to the children at the big house,' Angelo said. 'Mr Fisher was allowing him to live in one of the workers' cottages in return for drawing lessons. There were two rooms upstairs—one was where he painted, and the other where he slept. The cottage overlooked a poppy field.'

'It could be our poppy field. And maybe Alice was a maid at the big house,' Mariana said. 'I'll photograph these, if you don't mind writing up a translation later.'

'Of course.'

The rest of the summer was uneventful; and then Angelo found something odd.

'This one's from early September. After the harvest. Carulli says he's leaving Barrington under a bit of a cloud,' Angelo said.

'What did he do—fall out with Mr Fisher?' she asked.

'It doesn't say. Or maybe… If he fell in love with Alice, were they caught together and she was disgraced?' He shook his head and answered his own question. 'No, because the Fishers would've insisted that he marry her and he wouldn't have left—or at least he would've taken her back to Florence with him. He doesn't mention that at all.'

'This was 1863. Actually, he couldn't have

married her, because that would've made him a bigamist.' Mariana grimaced.

'He was already married?' Angelo looked at her, shocked.

'Yes.' She looked something up on the laptop. 'In 1863, he had three children. His daughter was born in winter 1862, so he'd left his pregnant wife in Florence while he went off on that painting trip in summer 1862, then he swanned off again the next summer, leaving her on her own with the baby and two small children.' She frowned. 'Sometimes these creative geniuses really weren't very nice and they didn't treat the people in their lives very well.'

Angelo wondered if she was thinking of Eric.

And he couldn't help thinking of Stephanie. She wasn't a creative genius, but she hadn't been willing to find a compromise—and she'd broken his heart.

And Carulli had just swanned off to paint and do whatever he pleased, ignoring his wife and small children. In his shoes… He felt a spark of anger at the painter's selfishness. 'How could he just leave his wife and kids like that? I mean, I understand that he was a creative genius and painting was what drove him, but how could he just leave his wife and kids?'

She looked surprised, and he remembered that she was supposed to think that he didn't care about children.

'Never mind,' he said. 'It's not meant to be about judging him. We need to find Alice.' He thought for a moment. 'Supposing it wasn't just being caught together in the Fishers' house? Supposing...?' Then he found he couldn't quite say the words that were in his head. It reminded him too much of the missing area in the middle of his life. What he couldn't have. What Carulli had had and treated so lightly.

'She was pregnant? That's a possibility,' she said. 'Is there anything in the letters about a baby, or paying for lying-in expenses, or anything like that?' she asked.

Angelo forced himself to damp down the longing and the loss, and work with his lawyer's head on. Dry facts. Not feelings. He scanned through the letters. 'Nothing. No further mentions of Barrington and nothing at all about Alice. He talks about his paintings and that's about it.'

'We need to look at other sources, then.' She frowned. 'Has the local history group got in touch with you yet?'

'No.' He looked at her. 'Maybe we need to do what Nonno did and visit the place ourselves, see if there's anything still there. I know it's half a century since Nonno visited, and a century more since Carulli was there, but if there's a big house then it's highly likely there's some kind of archive.' He gave her a wry smile. 'And hopefully they have a different attitude to filing than my grandfather does.'

She smiled back. 'Hopefully.'

When they got to the *palazzo*, Leo was frailer than the previous week but thrilled to see them, and he was even more thrilled when Angelo and Mariana handed over the package of what they'd found so far.

'Can you remember the name of the people at the big house?' Mariana asked. 'Was it Fisher?'

'I can't remember,' Leo said. 'So many things I should have asked them. But it was seeing the painting, seeing how nearly it was thrown away—all I could think of right then was rescuing it.'

'I found something else, Nonno,' Angelo said. 'Cine films from when you and Nonna were first married and when Mamma was small. I had them transferred to digital. Would you like to see them?'

'My Frederica?' Leo's eyes went misty.

Angelo played the films on his laptop, and Leo was actually in tears by the time they'd finished.

'I brought a copy for you on DVD, Nonno,' Angelo said. 'And I have copies for Mamma and Cammie.'

'You're a good boy,' Leo said. 'Steady, like your father was. I liked Roderick. He was good for my Lucrezia.'

'Not dramatic and arty, like you and Mamma, or even Cammie,' Angelo said. 'Mariana's been teaching me about art. It seems I like Turner and van Gogh and Degas.'

'Then there's hope for you yet,' Leo said. 'Teach him to love the Macchiaioli and my *Girl*, Mariana.'

'I'm working on it,' she said with a smile.

* * *

Leo perked up again the next morning, when Jeremy arrived, enthused over the collection as a whole and then stared at *The Girl in the Window* for a whole five minutes without saying a word.

'I—I'm lost for words,' he said, 'and Mariana will tell you that really doesn't happen very often.'

'But, because we don't have a signature and we don't have enough of a paper trail, yet,' Mariana said, 'we'll need to do tests on the painting.'

'Will you let us take your *Girl* to London, Nonno?' Angelo asked. 'I won't let it out of my sight between here and London, and I'll deliver it to the lab myself.'

'And the tests will prove it's Carulli?' Leo asked.

'I'd be astounded if they didn't,' Jeremy said. 'I've taught history of art for thirty-five years and my period is the nineteenth century. Professionally I'm considered an expert, and I'm pretty sure this is a Carulli. But, with all the forgery scandals in the art world, we need to go that step further than just my word.'

'Then take my *Girl*,' Leo said.

Mariana hugged him. 'Thank you. We'll take extra-special care of her.'

On the way back to London on Sunday, Angelo said, 'Jeremy's pulling strings and sorting out the lab for us so I'm delivering the painting there first thing on Monday morning.'

'Nigel's meeting us at the lab to see the picture for himself,' Mariana said.

'And then,' he said, 'I'm driving us to Norfolk and we'll see what we can find at Barrington. It might be an idea to take an overnight bag.'

'Because we might need to stay over, depending on what we find?' Mariana asked.

'Exactly.'

So in the middle of Monday morning—after Nigel had visited the painting and told Mariana it was going to be the star of the next series, whatever they found—they drove to Norfolk.

The cottages on New Road were still there; Mariana took a couple of shots of them. As Angelo had discovered on the Internet, the Red

Lion was now a private house. The farmhouse was just outside the village, down a long, narrow drive lined by lime trees.

'Let's go and see if the owners are in,' she said. 'If not, we can leave a note. I'm sure they'll be interested that their house is part of our mystery and they'll contact us.'

Even though her ex had crushed her belief in herself personally, Angelo thought, she believed in herself professionally. And that confidence made her shine.

This was strictly work, he reminded himself, and he parked on the gravel next to a large four-by-four, then followed Mariana to the front door and knocked.

A woman answered. 'Sorry, I don't buy at the door,' she said, looking wary. 'And the dogs aren't keen on strangers.'

There was a deep bark from behind her, to back up what she said.

'I'm not selling anything,' he said. 'My name's Angelo Beresford, and I'm a solicitor. This is Mariana Thackeray. We were wondering if you could help us with some information to try and track something down.'

'Mariana from *Hidden Treasure*! I love your programme,' the woman said. Her countenance changed completely. 'I wasn't expecting to see you on my doorstep!'

'I'm sorry we didn't write to you first, but we're checking out some hunches about a lost painting,' Mariana said. 'It belongs to Angelo's grandfather and I think your house might be a piece of the puzzle.'

'Come in and I'll put the kettle on. I'm Aggie Fryer,' she said. 'John, John, come and see who it is!'

Once they were settled with a cup of tea, and the two black Labradors had sprawled at Mariana's feet to have their tummies rubbed, Mariana explained about Carulli and showed the Fryers the photographs.

'That definitely looks like our house,' Aggie said.

'My grandfather visited the area when he bought the painting, back in 1963,' Angelo said. 'Did the house belong to your family?'

'No, we moved here ten years ago.' John said. He smiled at Angelo. 'Fancy our house being painted. Your grandfather doesn't want to sell the picture, does he?'

'I'm afraid not,' Angelo said.

'And, because it's you,' Aggie said, looking at Mariana, 'that means the painting's worth a lot more than everyone thinks it is, doesn't it?'

Mariana nodded. 'Sorry.'

'It's just—oh, my days. How amazing,' Aggie said.

'We bought the house from Billy Reynolds,' John said. 'He retired to a cottage in the middle of the village.'

'Do you know if he's still there?' Angelo asked.

'Sorry, I'm afraid we don't,' Aggie said.

'We're also looking for whatever would've been known as the big house,' Mariana said.

'Barrington Manor,' John said promptly. 'It's past the church on the other side of the village.'

'Do let us know what you find out,' Aggie said.

'We will,' Angelo promised.

Back in the car, he said to Mariana, 'You can do the knocking at the big house. You're the celebrity.'

She gave him a speaking look. 'Hardly. I've done sixteen television programmes over the last three years. I'm more of an art historian than a broadcaster.'

'But Aggie Fryer recognised you, and that's why she was willing to talk to us,' Angelo said.

'I guess.'

'And you're good with people,' he added. 'It makes sense to use our team's strengths.'

And how bad was it that the tiny spark of light in her eyes made him feel warm all over?

At Barrington Manor, the owners had the same reaction as the Fryers.

'Our house might be connected to a painting? Goodness,' Catherine James said.

'My grandfather bought it from the family who lived here fifty years ago,' Angelo said.

'Not mine, I'm afraid,' Catherine said. 'We moved here twenty years ago. I can't remember the name of the people who sold it—Peter, can you?'

'The Fishers,' her husband said.

Angelo exchanged a glance with Mariana. He could see the excitement in her face as she recognised the name. The same excitement that was fizzing through him—which also had a lot to do with Mariana being by his side, and he needed to get a grip.

'We can give you the name of their solicitor. They might be able to put you in touch,' Peter said.

'Thank you for your help,' Angelo said when Peter had found the details. Back at the car, he turned to Mariana. 'So close and so far. Now what do we do?'

'I guess we'll just have to knock on doors until we find Billy Reynolds,' she said.

They were halfway back to the village when Angelo's phone rang. He answered on the car's hands-free system. 'Angelo Beresford speaking.'

'Mr Beresford, it's Hattie Webster. You left me a message about the village history society.'

Angelo and Mariana exchanged a glance.

'Perfect timing,' she mouthed.

'Funnily enough, we're in Barrington right now,' Angelo said.

'Then do come and see me. I'd be delighted to help.' She gave them her address.

When they arrived, Hattie greeted them

warmly, and seemed thrilled to be part of the search behind the painting.

'Billy moved next door when he sold the farm,' she said. 'Though he moved to a residential home earlier in the year—he has arthritis and he was really struggling to manage on his own, and he refused flatly to move in with his daughters because he didn't want to be a burden, even though the two of them are lovely girls and wouldn't have minded a bit. But he's sharp as a tack and I'm sure he'll remember your grandfather, Angelo.' She wrote the address down for them. 'As for Alice, your best bet is to start with the census returns to see if she was anywhere in the village; and you could check the church records for births, deaths and marriages.'

'Are the records all online?' Angelo asked.

'The census records are, and the church records will be at the Records Office.' She scribbled down some information for them.

By the time they'd left Hattie, it was too late to call in at the residential home to see Billy Reynolds, or to go to the Records Office.

'It's pointless driving back to London and

then back here in the morning,' Angelo said. 'Let's stay overnight.'

'Good idea,' Mariana said. 'We can work out our revised research plan over dinner.'

He drove to the nearest market town and booked two rooms at a former coaching inn. But, when they went up to find their rooms after dinner, Mariana's key refused to work in the door.

'I'll come down with you to sort it out,' Angelo said.

When Mariana asked for another key, the receptionist was apologetic. 'I'm so sorry, Miss Thackeray. There's been a mix-up—I'm afraid that room was already reserved tonight, which is why your key didn't work, and we're full with a wedding. That room your friend booked was the last one we had.'

Angelo looked at Mariana. 'We could try to find somewhere else.'

She shook her head. 'It's getting late. Look, we're both adults. If you don't mind, we can share your room.'

Share his room. He'd really need to keep his feelings under control. Bury the longing. Because he couldn't offer her the future he knew she wanted.

'OK. But I'll sleep on the floor,' he said on the way up to his room.

'I might be a student, but I'm definitely too old to sleep on the floor—and so are you,' she said. 'The bed's wide enough for us to share.'

Angelo was very, very aware of her beside him, and he was very, very careful to make sure he kept space between them, even though what he really wanted to do was to wrap his arms round her and kiss her until they were both dizzy. He closed his eyes and thought of knotty legal problems, pretending to be asleep until Mariana's own breathing was deep and even. Then he lay there with his eyes open, wishing things were different. That he'd never had mumps. And he knew how pointless his wishes were.

Somehow he fell asleep; but then he woke up in the middle of the night with her arms wrapped round him and his wrapped round her.

Her breathing wasn't deep or even enough

for her to be asleep. Which meant she was awake. Aware of what she was doing.

What was she thinking?

'Mariana,' he whispered, unable to help himself.

'Sorry. I should…' She wriggled out of his arms. 'My fault.'

'It's just as much mine,' he said softly. 'I'm sorry if you thought I was making a move on you.'

'I'm sorry if you thought I was making a move on *you*,' she said.

'I wish you were.'

And then he realised he'd spoken aloud. Of all the stupid, insane things to have said…

'Forget I said that,' he said swiftly.

Angelo had just said he wished she was making a move on him. How could she ignore that? Her heart was racing hard enough as if she'd just run a five-k at a personal best. 'I can't.'

'I apologise.'

Something in his tone alerted her. What was it that her sister had said? A fling. Right now, that seemed like the best idea in the world. All she had to do was be brave. Take the risk. Ask for what she wanted.

'Maybe I don't want you to apologise.'

'Are you saying…?'

It was so much easier to say this in the cocoon of the dark. Where she didn't have to meet his eyes and feel awkward or embarrassed, where she could let the tone of his voice guide her. She took a deep breath. 'Neither of us is looking for a relationship. You're divorced and I'm still licking my wounds from Eric. And we're working together to solve a mystery for your grandfather and prove that painting is what he thinks it is.'

'It would be utterly insane for us to get involved with each other,' he agreed. Which sounded more like he was saying he thought it was a perfect idea.

'Utterly,' she said, hoping he was reading her tone, too. Just in case he wasn't, she stroked his face.

He turned his head so his mouth skimmed against her palm. 'Mariana, I haven't been able to stop thinking about you since I first met you.'

He'd said it first. Which made everything easier. 'I can't stop thinking about you, too,' she admitted.

'So maybe,' he said, 'maybe we should get this out of our systems. To let us concentrate on work tomorrow.'

'A fling.'

'A fling,' he agreed. 'Just tonight.'

'Because then we'll know how ridiculous this is and we don't have a future,' she said.

'Absolutely.' He brushed his mouth against hers.

'An excellent plan.' She kissed him back.

'Just tonight and then we'll forget all about it,' he said.

'Agreed.'

Making love should've been awkward and difficult and embarrassing; but it felt so right. Afterwards, he curled protectively round her, holding her close. As she drifted off to sleep, she felt more at peace than she had in years.

Tomorrow they'd be back to being professional.

But she was glad they'd had tonight.

CHAPTER EIGHT

ON THE TUESDAY MORNING, Angelo woke before Mariana.

Last night had been a mistake. A huge mistake. They'd agreed that it would be just for that night, that it was just to get all the inappropriate stuff out of their systems, and this morning they would be back to being professional.

The problem was, it hadn't worked. All the inappropriate feelings were still there. If anything, it was worse—because now he knew how it felt to hold her. How it felt to kiss her. How it felt to make love with her. And he didn't want to stop.

But at the same time he knew it wouldn't be fair to her to ask her to make it a real relationship. Not when she wanted things he knew he couldn't give her. A family. A future.

How were they going to deal with this?

He hadn't had any good ideas by the time she woke up.

'Good morning,' she said softly, and her smile made him feel warm all over—and guilty as hell at the same time. He couldn't lie to her, couldn't pretend they could make a go of things and then let her down. He had to do the right thing. End it. Now.

'Good morning.' He took a deep breath. 'We need to talk about last night.'

Her smile vanished, and he hated himself for what he was about to do. But better to do it now than to leave it until they both got badly hurt. He needed to think of it like ripping off a plaster. Do it quickly, so you didn't prolong the agony.

'We agreed that it was just going to be that. Last night,' he said.

'Uh-huh.' Her expression was completely impassive, but he knew he'd hurt her.

'I'm sorry,' he said, raking his hand through his hair. 'I took advantage of you.'

'We took advantage of each other,' she corrected.

'But I wasn't fair to you. I...'

'You made me feel like an attractive woman for the first time in years,' she said softly, and colour stained her cheekbones.

Guilt surged through him even more. Hadn't she already told him how hard she was finding it to start another relationship? And now he was knocking her back, making her feel useless and hopeless and unattractive again. He'd been so unfair to her. 'You *are* an attractive woman. But we can't do this. Mariana. *I* can't do this.'

She said nothing, but her face was the tiniest bit pinched.

'It's not you,' he said. 'It's me. I can't...' He owed it to her to tell her the truth. 'You said you wanted children,' he said.

'At some point, yes,' she agreed.

When she met the right man. Who so wasn't him. 'I can't do that.'

'Because you don't want children.'

Oh, but he did. He'd had such plans for the future. And they'd all turned to dust. Yes, he had his niece, who would also be his goddaughter. But that wouldn't have been enough for Stephanie. It wouldn't be enough for any woman who wanted a child of her own.

'I can't have children,' he said. 'That's why Stephanie left me. Why we got divorced. I had mumps when I was young, and it left me infertile.'

Mariana said nothing.

He didn't want to see pity in her eyes, so he didn't look at her. He should never, ever have given in to his body's urging last night. Hadn't he learned that he wasn't *enough*? 'So it's pointless getting involved with me, because I can't give you what you want.'

'So you do want children.'

Wasn't she listening? That wasn't the issue. 'I can't have them,' he repeated.

'There's more to being a parent than biology,' she said softly. 'There's adoption. Fostering.'

Things he'd suggested to Stephanie and she'd rejected out of hand. 'Or IVF.' The words came out before he could stop them.

'Or IVF,' she said.

He looked at her, then. And there was no pity in her face. No judgement. Just sympathy. But he couldn't do this. Couldn't take the risk. Couldn't face everything collapsing round him again.

'I wasn't enough for Stephanie. I know you're not her, but I just can't open myself up to that sort of hurt again.' Being found wanting. Rejected. 'I'm sorry. I wish things could be different. Last night, I should never—'

'I get it,' she cut in. 'We shouldn't have slept together. It was a mistake. And I understand if you'd rather have someone else work on your grandfather's paintings. I can give you a few names.'

He raked his hand through his hair. 'No. That isn't fair. You've done so much already.' How could he take this away from her, knowing how much she loved Carulli's work? Or was this her way of telling him she wanted out? He faced it head-on. 'Unless you'd rather not work with me any more.'

'I want to know the story behind the painting,' she said. 'I want to do the cataloguing and study the paintings for my thesis.'

'So you can work with me? Even though...' Even though they'd made the mistake of sleeping together?

'As long as we keep things strictly professional from here on,' she said.

Which made it very clear to him that she didn't feel quite the same way that he did, wishing things could be different, because she wasn't trying to fight him and argue that maybe they had a chance together. It was obvious that last night, for her, had been an aberration. And she was happy to go back to how they'd been before: because she was bright enough to work out that he wouldn't be enough for her, just as he hadn't been enough for Stephanie.

They were doing the right thing. Even if it did make him feel miserable.

'You have the bathroom first,' he said, desperately wanting some space. And then he'd have a really cold shower to hammer it through his stupid skull never to give in to his emotions and his desires ever, ever again.

Was he pushing her away because he was infertile? Mariana wondered. Or was he using his infertility as an excuse—because Eric was right about her after all and nobody would really want to saddle themselves with someone like her?

Or maybe it was both.

How stupid she'd been, letting him get close to her and thinking that maybe he felt the same way that she did, wanting a relationship yet being scared it would all go wrong. Saying one thing with his mouth and another with his body. She'd been foolish enough to believe that their shared lovemaking had actually meant something. But, yet again, she'd managed to pick a man who couldn't love her for who she was.

Well, she'd definitely learned her lesson, this time. She'd keep all her relationships professional, in future. But she wasn't going to let all her dreams slide into nothingness. She was going to find out the truth behind Leo Moretti's painting and she was going to work on cataloguing his collection. Angelo might not want her as a woman, but she knew he appreciated her work. And work was what would get her through this. Just as it had got her through the misery of Eric's behaviour.

After an awkward breakfast, they bought a

tin of biscuits for Billy, then headed for the residential home where he lived. Angelo was scrupulously polite and professional and again Mariana regretted giving in to the impulse last night. Why hadn't she kept her distance?

Billy Reynolds was pleased with his gift but he was even more pleased with the company. 'I love your programme, Miss Thackeray. The way you follow the trail all the way back from people who don't have a clue about what they have, and then they find out their painting's worth a small fortune. But I don't know anything about paintings, so I don't really know how I can help you.'

'My grandfather bought a painting which shows the house you used to live in.' Angelo showed Billy the photographs of Leo at the manor, the painting, and the photograph Leo had taken of Manor Farm.

'That's Manor Farm, all right. And I remember your grandfather visiting. I must've been in my teens back then.' Billy looked thoughtful. 'So he found the painting up at the big house?'

'Yes. We were wondering what the connection might be between the farm and the manor,' Mariana said.

Billy shook his head. 'No idea. My family had that farm for generations before me. I don't know of any connection with the big house, other than the name.'

'We think the woman in the painting might be called Alice,' Mariana said. 'Is she one of your relatives?'

He squinted at the photograph. 'She looks a bit like my grandfather's younger sister, but I don't think she was called Alice.'

With Billy being in his seventies now, even if they allowed thirty years for each generation, his great-aunt's generation would still have been born well after the date of the painting.

'I should have asked my mum to write the names on the back of all the old photos. Shirley, my oldest daughter, is researching the family tree and every so often she brings down a bunch of photos and gets me to tell her what I can remember.' Billy paused. 'I could ask her to get in touch with you.'

'That would be really kind. Thank you,' Angelo said, giving Billy his card.

The next stop was the solicitor's office in Norwich.

'I'm afraid that information is confidential,' the receptionist told them when Angelo asked about the Fishers. 'Under the data protection laws, I can't confirm or deny anything.'

Angelo handed her his business card. 'I understand completely. But I was hoping you could ask them to call us.' He explained about the painting. 'Anything they say to us will be in the strictest confidence.'

'I know it's a bit above and beyond the call of duty,' Mariana said, 'but Angelo's grandfather has lung cancer and we'd really like to solve this for him before...' She stopped and grimaced.

The receptionist's face softened. 'I lost my grandfather to cancer. It's a horrible disease. All right. I'll see what I can do.'

'Thank you,' Mariana said.

'Do you have time to go to the Records Office?' Angelo asked as they left the building.

'We might as well. Two pairs of eyes are quicker than one.' And, the quicker they wrapped up this project, the quicker she'd be out of his way. The quicker she'd be able to build up the protective layers around her heart again.

At the Records Office, they talked to the staff about where to find the information they wanted, and finally they sat down with one of the computer terminals to look up the local census records.

'Eighteen sixty-one, Barrington, Norfolk,' she said.

They scrolled through the pages. 'Here's New Road. None of the families living in the cottages are the Reynoldses or the Fishers,' she said. 'But here's Manor Farm. *"Robert Reynolds, aged thirty-eight, tenant farmer and widower."'*

They continued searching. 'Here's Barrington Manor. *"Charles Fisher, aged forty-eight, land proprietor,"'* Angelo read. '*"Wife Harriet, aged forty-six; sons Henry, Frederick, James—"* And, oh, look at this.'

"'Alice, daughter, aged fifteen, scholar,"' Mariana read.

'That's 1861. So when Carulli comes to the village for the first time, the year after, she's sixteen. The second time, when his letter to his brother says he's got a job as the drawing master for Mr Fisher's children, she's seventeen.'

They looked at each other. 'Alice is the daughter of the house, not the servant we assumed she was. No wonder Carulli left the village under a cloud, if he had a fling with her. She was his pupil,' Mariana said.

Alice had fallen in love with the wrong person. Mariana knew how that felt. She'd made a similar mistake. Alice had fallen in love with someone who wasn't free to love her back; Mariana was falling for someone who was too stubborn to let himself love her back. Someone who'd closed himself off to everyone.

She shook herself. This wasn't about her and Angelo. They needed to work together, for Leo's sake. Find the truth.

If only they could negotiate the minefield of their pasts and their mistakes as easily.

'So what happened to Alice?' he asked.

Had she stayed in Barrington, lonely and sad, eating her heart out over the artist who'd made her light up in that portrait? Or had she managed to move on with her life?

'Let's try the 1871 census,' she suggested.

'Charles and Harriet are still there at the manor, but no mention of Alice or her brothers,' he said. 'So is Alice still alive? Did she marry someone else and move away, too?'

'And what's the connection with the farmhouse?' Mariana asked.

'Let's look at Manor Farm again.' He raised his eyebrows. 'Robert's sons have all married and moved into cottages. Robert's listed as a farmer, but there's nothing about being a tenant, and—oh, my God. Look at the next line.'

'"*Wife, Alice, aged twenty-five,*"' Mariana said softly. 'The same age as Alice Fisher would be.'

'So is that our Alice? And they have a son, Thomas. Aged seven.'

'Born in 1864,' Mariana said, 'which means he was conceived in 1863.'

They looked at each other. 'So this could be our Alice,' Angelo said.

'So is Thomas's father Carulli rather than Robert Reynolds?' she asked.

'There's a big age gap between Robert and Alice. More than twenty years. How likely is it that the only daughter of the family at the big house is going to marry one of her father's tenant farmers?' Angelo asked. 'Surely her parents would want to marry her off to a son of a neighbouring rich family and consolidate the family fortune?'

'She wouldn't have had much say in the matter, back then,' Mariana said. 'She wouldn't have had much choice in anything.'

He flinched slightly, as if seeing the similarities with their own situation. He wasn't giving her any choice. And Mariana wanted to grab his shoulders and shake him and yell at him for being so ridiculously stubborn. Why couldn't he see that not every woman had the same views as his ex? Why couldn't he see that they had a real chance of making a go of things?

Then again, who was she to talk, when she found it hard to trust? She bit back her impatience. 'Let's look at the church records.'

'Alice should be in 1846—yes, she's here,' Angelo said. 'Listed with her mother Harriet and her father Charles.'

'Here's Thomas Reynolds, in March 1864.'

Mariana worked backwards. 'So he was conceived in June 1863, and Alice would've known for definite by September that she was pregnant. It all ties up.'

'So was the baby Carulli's? Or did she fall in love with Robert and have a secret fling with him rather than Carulli, and maybe Carulli took the blame?' Angelo asked.

'Would a seventeen-year-old girl really fall for someone twice her age—someone who's not far off the age of her own father—and not from the same social class as her family? If she'd fallen for one of Robert's sons, I could imagine that more easily,' Mariana said.

'Let's see if we can find the wedding,' Angelo said.

They pored over the screen together; the tiny space meant that they were jammed up against each other. *Touching.* Angelo was very, very aware of Mariana: the warmth of her body, her light floral scent. He couldn't help thinking about last night. How it had felt to sleep with Mariana in his arms. How wonderful. How right. Maybe he could tell her he'd made a mistake in pushing her away—but how selfish that would be. How could he expect her to give up her dreams of a family for him?

He really needed to get a grip.

They were looking up information about the woman who was possibly the model in his grandfather's painting. And his feelings about Mariana needed to be squashed. Right now.

'Here we go. *"Robert Reynolds of this parish, widower, aged forty, and Alice Fisher of this parish, spinster, aged seventeen. Married by licence in this church, the first of October 1863,"*' she read.

'What does "married by licence" mean?' he asked.

She looked it up on the Internet. 'You didn't have to have the banns read. So it was a rushed wedding, by the sounds of it. Oh, look—she's signed the register, but Robert has put a cross, with the vicar's handwriting next to it saying *"his mark".*'

'So she could write and he couldn't.'

'I hope,' she said softly, 'he didn't make her feel bad about that.'

Was she thinking about the way Eric had

made her feel bad about herself? Or—guilt flooded through him—was she thinking about the way Angelo himself had made her feel? 'They might have been happy together,' he said. 'She might have taught him to write.'

'I hope so.'

He continued looking at the file. 'Robert's father was Thomas—he's deceased. So I'm guessing that Robert took over from him at the farm. And Alice's father is Charles Fisher, landowner. So she's definitely our Alice. Her father is a witness, along with John Reynolds—Robert's oldest son.'

She bit her lip. 'It looks to me as if Charles did a deal with one of his tenants—marry Alice and give the baby his name, and in return he'd get the farm. Let's check and see if they had any more children.' She went back to the microfiche for the births and scrolled through the rest of the eighteen-seventies. 'No. No more children. So maybe Robert and Alice agreed that it would be a marriage in name only. Or maybe they couldn't—' She stopped. 'Sorry.'

Angelo flinched. He knew what she'd been about to say, and he knew just how that felt.

Would Robert have wanted children of his own with his new young wife? Would he have wanted a daughter, perhaps, with her mother's beautiful smile? As the years passed, and no children arrived, would he have felt more and more useless, less and less of a man, the way Angelo himself had felt after Stephanie's rejection? Or would Robert have been content with the three sons he'd had with his first wife? How would it feel to bring up someone else's child as your own?

Stephanie had refused to consider IVF. Or adoption. Or fostering. But Mariana had brought up the subject herself.

Could they…?

He squashed the hope. It was one thing suggesting it and quite another going through with it.

'Angelo, I didn't mean—'

'I know,' he cut in, a little more brusquely than he should have done.

She stared at him. 'You don't have to snap.'

'Sorry,' he muttered.

'You don't sound it.' She frowned. 'Don't take out your bad mood on me. That's not fair.'

It was what Eric had done, and that made Angelo feel guilty enough to snap back, 'No, and not being able to have children isn't fair, either.'

'I know,' she said, her voice very quiet, 'and I feel for you. Not pity—sympathy, and there's a big difference. But I think you're wallowing in it and using it as an excuse not to make any effort.'

'What?' He stared at her in disbelief. She was accusing him of *wallowing* in the thing that had ripped his life apart?

'Not every woman's going to react like your ex. But I guess it's easier to shut yourself away from everyone than to have the guts to try again.'

She was absolutely right, and that made his temper flare. 'Says the woman who won't trust her own judgement.'

She didn't deny it. But she put her hands on her hips and glared at him. 'At least I'm trying.'

'Are you?' That wasn't what she'd said to him.

'I tried,' she said, 'with you. But you're too obstinate to consider anything but your own point of view. You're pig-headed, and you're so *wrong* it's untrue.'

'I'm trying to do the right thing for you. You want children and I can't have them, so there's no point in us getting together because we'll just let each other down.'

'So why did you sleep with me last night?'

He had to take that one on the chin. Own up to what he'd done. 'Because I was being selfish.' And, actually, so was she. 'But *you* agreed it was just for one night. Now you're changing the terms.'

'No, now I'm being honest with myself and admitting that I want more than just a fling—that I'm *worth* more than that. And it's OK to admit that.'

'Is it?'

Her eyes widened. 'Are you telling me you're trying to be noble?'

'You want children and I can't give you what you want—so, yes, I suppose I am. You're free to find someone who can give you what you want.'

'Like Stephanie did?' She shook her head. 'You know I'm not her. How stubborn and blinkered can you get? You're just making us both miserable with your refusal to see anything other than your point of view. Ironically, you're the one who showed me that I'm worth more—but you won't give me more. You're using your infertility as an excuse.'

'I'm not a coward.'

'I'm not saying that. Angelo. I'm saying it's not a weakness to admit you want something.'

'Even if you can't have it?' He curled his lip. 'That's just pointless. Crying for the moon.'

'Even if you *think* you can't have it,' she corrected. 'Because you can work round things. Because not everyone has the same views as your ex. For what it's worth, I think she was incredibly selfish and you're worth more than that.' She took a deep breath. 'But you're the one being selfish now. You're not considering what I might want.'

'Are you considering what *I* might want?' he countered.

'Yes. But if you're not prepared to be honest about it, there's no point in having this conversation.' She shook her head. 'You know what? I need some space from you. If it wasn't for the fact I promised your grandfather I'd find out the truth about the painting for him, I'd walk out on the job right now.'

'Then walk out,' he said. Hurt made him lash out and he added, 'Just like Stephanie did.' Mariana reckoned she wasn't the same as his ex, but right now she was doing exactly the same thing.

'I,' she said, narrowing her eyes at him, 'will make my own way home.'

He shook his head. 'Don't be ridiculous. We're miles away, in Norwich, and we're not even in the city centre.'

She glared at him. 'Did it not occur to you that this poor, silly, pathetic little woman might just be capable of calling a taxi to take her to the train station and buying a ticket?'

'What?' She was escalating this way over the top. 'I never called you silly or pathetic or little.'

'You implied it.'

'Like hell I did.' He rolled his eyes. 'You're being totally unreasonable. I'm not Eric.'

And I'm not Stephanie,' she said, in a whisper so harsh that it cut right through him. 'Think about it. Think long and hard about what you really want. And about whether you've got the guts to go and find it.'

And, to his shock, she stood up.

She really *was* walking out on him.

'Mariana—'

'No,' she cut in. 'Right now, I don't want to talk to you, Angelo. I'm going back to London on my own. I'll see you tomorrow to carry on with the paperwork, but I want you to know that I'm doing it for your grandfather, not for you.'

'Noted,' he said tightly.

'Good. My overnight bag is still in your car. I'll collect it from you tomorrow.' She looked at him. 'Think about what I said. Because it's way past time you stopped hiding.'

And then she walked away.

Angelo watched her go. Part of him wanted to call her back, part of him wanted to go after her, and part of him was too numb to do anything.

Was she right?

Was he wallowing in his infertility?

Was he too much of a coward to put himself

back out there and go for what he wanted—for what he knew he couldn't have?

The collapse of his marriage had hurt him so deeply. Why would anyone want to open themselves up to that kind of hurt again? And what was the point of wanting something you couldn't have?

But Alice Fisher had done it. She'd married a man who was beneath her social class and who wasn't the father of her child. A man who'd given her his name and his protection in exchange for becoming the owner of his farm. A man who had complete power over her, after their marriage. She'd taken a risk that Robert could make her life and that of her child really unhappy.

But had that been the case?

Robert had taken a risk, too. Marrying a woman way above his station, a woman who could read and write and who was used to having servants. A woman who might look down on him and make him feel unworthy of her.

But the facts were on the records from all those years ago. Robert had the farm and Alice kept her baby. Between them they'd been brave enough to make a compromise work.

Could he be that brave?

Out of habit—and respect for the fact that other people needed to use the library and it wasn't fair just to leave everything in a mess—he put all the microfiches and rolls of microfilm back in their right place. Then he drove to the train station to find Mariana, apologise and tell her that he was ready to talk.

But she wasn't there.

The departures board showed that there were half-hourly trains to London—and the last one had left three minutes ago.

He was too late.

CHAPTER NINE

MARIANA SAT ON the train, staring out of the window but not actually seeing anything of the pretty countryside.

What had she done?

She'd given in to her anger and her frustration. Walked out on Angelo, just as Stephanie had. The parallels weren't lost on her.

Had she been unfair?

Probably, and guilt flooded through her. He couldn't have children. They'd been chasing down the true story behind the painting, discovered that the painter had just abandoned his children when it suited him—his wife and children in Florence, and then Alice in Norfolk. Carulli had been cavalier in the extreme with the one thing Angelo wanted and couldn't have.

So a lot of what he'd said to her... His head

had been in a bad place. Maybe he hadn't meant any of it. And she'd hurt him.

But he'd rejected her, too. He wouldn't even discuss alternatives.

Was it her? Was Eric right and she was worthless, and no man would love her?

She shook herself. No. She wasn't worthless. But maybe she had a habit of picking men who simply weren't able to love.

Where they went from here, she had no idea. She'd finish the job: apart from her professional pride, she liked Leo Moretti and genuinely wanted to help him. But she and Angelo would be strangers—and it would stay that way.

What a fool she'd been. Hadn't she even said to Sophie that neither of them was the kind of person who did flings? He'd given her the opportunity to back away and she should've taken it. Yes, things might have been a bit awkward for a while, but they would've got over it eventually. Whereas this… It was pretty final. And very obvious that he wasn't prepared to give them a chance.

* * *

Angelo realised there was nothing further he could do here, so he drove back to London. Although he really wanted to talk to Mariana, and he was tempted to drive to her place and sit on her doorstep until she came home, she'd asked him for space—and she'd asked him to think about what he really wanted.

He knew the answer already. He wanted *her*. But he needed to be sure that he would be enough for her.

But if she could be brave enough to face the fear, so could he.

And he needed to respect her wishes and give her space. Her ex had bullied her; Angelo didn't want her to think he was out of the same mould. So, much as all his instincts screamed at him to go after her, he went back to his house.

How empty it seemed. Blank walls everywhere—like his life had been. Mariana had opened his eyes to art. Brought colour into his world. Now everything was back to being neat and tidy and colourless. Silent. Even the clock didn't tick: the hands moved silently. There was nothing to fill the spaces except for his regrets. And fear. If he was completely honest with her, would she give him a chance? Or would all the potential difficulties scare her away?

To take his mind off the situation, he went back to translating his grandfather's diaries. It felt odd to be working in his office without Mariana there. Over the last few weeks he'd got used to sharing his space with her, and he missed her. Several times he picked up the phone to call her; but then he put it down again. He didn't want to be like her ex and browbeat her into doing what he wanted. He wanted her to be with him because it was where *she* wanted to be, not because he'd talked her into it.

And she'd said she would see him in the morning. So he'd be patient and give her space to think and cool down. Even though it was killing him, because he wanted the rest of his life to start right now.

The next morning, it got to ten o'clock and she still hadn't arrived. Had she walked out on him for good? Had he completely misread the situation after all and she'd actually expected him to go after her yesterday, so the fact he hadn't made her think he didn't want her? Or—a nasty thought struck him—had something happened to her, an accident, and she hadn't made it home at all?

He'd been as careless with her as Carulli had been with Alice, and he didn't like himself for that.

He was about to call her to check that she was all right and ask if she'd agree to meet him on neutral ground, just to talk, when he realised it was Wednesday. The day she usually met with her tutor. She was probably at the university right now, and he was completely overreacting. Which so wasn't him. He was known for being cool, calm and rational at work. Right now, he felt like a hot-headed teenager, all over the place.

Was it really only a week ago that Mariana had taken him to meet Jeremy and then to the National and teased him into responding to the art? It felt like a lifetime ago. So much had changed since then. A week ago, he'd found himself hot all over, wondering what it would feel like to make love with her, cross with himself for letting his feelings get out of control in a public place, and more aware of her than he'd been of any woman—including Stephanie.

And now he knew exactly how it felt to make love with her. How warm and sweet and amazing she was. Why had he been so stupid? Why hadn't he actually listened to what she'd said about wanting more than just a fling, instead of trying to be noble pushing her away? Why hadn't he told her that it was what he wanted, too—that he knew he came with complications but he'd move heaven and earth to make things work?

When the phone rang, he snatched it up, hoping it was it Mariana telling him she was on her way. 'Hello?'

'Mr Beresford?'

He didn't recognise the voice and had to damp down his disappointment. 'Yes.'

'I'm Shirley Peters, Bill Reynolds's daughter. He said you wanted to talk to me about our family history.'

Mariana ought to be here for this conversation, he thought. Or maybe this would be his excuse to talk to her if she stonewalled him, and he could open the conversation by telling her of any new developments. 'Thank you so much for calling,' he said, and filled her in on what they'd found about the painting so far.

'So what did you want to know?' she asked.

'We're trying to find out more about Alice. Is she related to you?'

'She's my four-times great-grandmother,' Shirley confirmed. 'I can email the family tree over to you, if you like.'

'That,' Angelo said, 'would be fantastic.'

'I've got some copies of birth and marriage certificates, too,' she said.

'If you've got Alice and Robert's marriage certificate, and Thomas's birth certificate, I'd love to see them.'

'I'll scan them in and email them with the family tree,' she said.

'Thank you so much. And I can send you what we have,' Angelo said. 'We have photos of a sketch and a painting we think might be Alice. Our theory is that Carulli and Alice fell in love when he was her drawing teacher, they had an affair, and Thomas was the result.

Carulli was already married so he couldn't marry her, and we think Alice's father might have given Robert the farm in return for marrying Alice and saving her from scandal.'

'That would explain something in Dad's old papers—the farm's always gone to the oldest son, but Thomas was the *youngest* son. So if the farm belonged to Alice's family before she married Robert, maybe this was their way of making sure the land stayed with Alice's bloodline, starting with Thomas and then to the eldest son,' Shirley said thoughtfully.

'Do you have any family papers—letters or diaries?' Angelo asked hopefully.

'Nothing as far back as that, I'm afraid,' Shirley said. 'But I'll look through what I have, and I'll let you know if there's anything relevant.'

'Thank you. I really appreciate it.'

He'd just finished sending Shirley an email with photographs of the sketches and a rough written version of their theory when the doorbell rang.

He glanced at his watch.

Mariana.

Time to talk things through, to tell her how

he really felt—and please, please, let her want the same things that he did.

He took the stairs two at a time and flung the door open.

'Hi.'

Was it his imagination, or did she look nervous? 'Come in,' he said. And how ridiculous that every single word seemed to have gone out of his head. He couldn't just throw his arms round her and kiss her and tell her that he loved her. She'd think he'd gone crazy. But he couldn't just stand there and say nothing, either. 'I...' He noticed the dark shadows beneath her eyes. She'd obviously slept as badly as he had, last night. 'Are you OK?'

'Yes. Sorry, my tutorial meeting overran.'

'Uh-huh.' He took a deep breath. 'I'm sorry about yesterday, Mariana. About losing my temper and yelling at you. And I'm not being insincere—I know I hurt you and I'm truly sorry.'

'Apology accepted.'

Though her tone was utterly neutral and he couldn't tell what was going through her head. Did she really forgive him or was she still angry with him? Accepting an apology wasn't the same thing as saying everything was OK between them; or maybe he was just getting tangled in lawyerly semantics. 'Can we talk?' he asked.

She paused for so long that he thought she was going to say no, but then she nodded.

He ushered her into the kitchen and gestured to her to sit down at the table. 'Coffee?'

'No, thanks.'

Her expression said it for her: she knew he was trying to put off the moment when he finally opened up to her. Time to stop prevaricating and be brave. He sat down opposite her. 'I wanted to come after you yesterday. But then I thought of what you'd been through with Eric and I didn't want you to feel bullied. I wanted you to see that I'd respect your wishes, that I'd give you space when you asked for it.'

He really couldn't read the expressions skittering over her face. Was she relieved, hurt, pleased? A mixture?

He pressed on. 'What you said yesterday, about me wallowing in my infertility...' The word stuck in his throat.

'Sorry, that wasn't very fair of me.'

'It wasn't kind and it hurt,' he said, acknowledging that she'd made him feel bad. 'But it was true. I *have* been wallowing. I've been so caught up in thinking about what a failure I was as a husband, how I wasn't enough for Stephanie—but you've been through something worse and you picked yourself up and made yourself carry on, whereas I just retreated into my work and kept myself too busy to feel anything.'

'That,' she said, 'sounds painfully honest.'

'Facing the truth hurts,' he admitted. 'But it's the only way forward. And you were right. I needed to think about it. To think about what I want from life. What's important to me.'

She went very still. 'And do you have any answers?'

'Yes.' He looked levelly at her. 'I'm a corporate lawyer. Facts I can do. But I find talking about emotions difficult. I don't know if it's because Mamma's so dramatic that I kind of went to the opposite extreme, or if it's a bloke thing, or… It's just…' He shook his head. 'And I'm not usually this inarticulate.' He gave her a wry smile. 'It's important I get this right, but I'm making a mess of it.'

She reached across the table and took his hand. 'You don't have to start at the beginning or even make sense. The important thing is to start—and it can go on from there. Find its own way of coming out.'

Her voice was so kind, so gentle. Letting him know that she wasn't going to judge him. Or at least not judge him as harshly as he judged himself. As harshly as Stephanie had judged him.

If he told her what was in his head and she backed away, it couldn't make things any worse than they'd been last night, when she'd walked out on him. They'd still be apart. But if she didn't back away now...

Hope began to flicker inside him.

'I'm good at my job,' he said. 'I sort out mergers, I sort out buy-outs, and I make sure all the staff are treated fairly.' He blew out a breath. 'I love my family. I'm there when they need me. But I was a total failure as a husband. I made a mess of my marriage. I wasn't enough for Stephanie—and the idea of putting myself through that again, taking the risk and getting it wrong and being rejected and abandoned… That scares the hell out of me.'

'Taking a risk is hard,' she said. 'You were the first man I let close to me since Eric. There was just something about you. The way you made me feel. That you valued me, valued my knowledge, and made me feel that I was worth something.'

'You *are* worth something. A lot. More than I can give you,' he said. 'I know you're not Stephanie. That you can see there's more than one way to make a family. But it scares me that I'll let you down, too. That maybe we can't make a family, and I won't be enough for you.'

'The way I see it, we have two options,' she said. 'We can both stay scared—you scared that you won't be enough for me and I'll reject you, and me scared that I've picked Mr Wrong again and you'll make me feel worthless.' She paused. 'Or we can both be brave and take a risk together.'

'Trust our own judgement?'

'Or maybe trust each other's judgement,' she said. 'What do you really want, Angelo?'

'You,' he said. 'I want you. I want what my parents had. Someone who loves me for who I am, someone who brings light and colour into my life. Someone whose dreams I can support, someone who's my equal, someone who'll share the tough times as well as the good.' He took a deep breath. 'And a family. Even though that's not going to be easy, thanks to the mumps—and whatever we do, whether we foster or adopt or try IVF, it's going to take time.'

She looked at him. 'I come with complications, too. Eric and the injunction. Will that stand in the way of us being able to adopt or foster?'

'I don't know,' he admitted. 'Family law isn't my area. But I have friends who would be able to answer that—friends who'd be able to fight our corner if we needed help.' He tightened his hands round hers. 'I want to make a family with you, Mariana.'

'That's what I want, too,' she said. 'But what if we can't?'

He took a deep breath. 'You have a nephew. I have a niece. So we'll still have children in our closest family. We'll still be able to watch the next generation grow up and share their lives.'

'Is that going to be enough for you?' she asked.

He looked at her. 'If I have you by my side, then yes. You're enough for me. What about you?'

'You're enough for me, too,' she said softly.

Thank God, he thought. His complications hadn't scared her away. And hers most definitely didn't scare him. 'I don't want to hurt you,' he said.

'You won't,' she said.

'I hurt you yesterday,' he pointed out.

'We hurt each other. I think we're going to have to learn to manage fights a bit better and talk properly instead of me stomping off and you sulking,' she said ruefully.

'Agreed.'

'But you're not someone who hurts people for the sake of it. Remember when I broke that mug? You lifted me up and carried me away from anything that could hurt me, you brought ice to cool the burn on my hand, and you fetched my shoes so I didn't have to rely on you carrying me anywhere because you know I value my independence. You kept me safe,' she said. 'And that's why I know you won't hurt me. That I can trust you. That I'll keep my independence but you'll be there when I need you.' She swallowed hard. 'And I hope that working with me has taught you that you can trust me. That I'll be there when you need me.'

There when he needed her.

And he knew she would be. Just as he would be there for her.

'You bring colour into my life,' he said. 'You make me see things differently. My house is all wrong. It's not a home. There's a difference between having clutter, the way Nonno does, and having more than blank walls. My house needs paintings. It needs *you*.' He paused. 'Not just my house. *I* need you. That day you took me to the National—I think that's when I fell in love with you. Your warmth. Your brightness. It scares me to hell that you've made me feel things again. But I think I can be brave, with you by my side. I can reach for the happiness because, even though life won't always be easy or simple, it'll be there. I love you, Mariana.'

'When you pushed me away yesterday... I hated feeling not good enough.'

'I'm sorry I hurt you. My head was all over the place. That's not an excuse—it's an explanation. I love you and I didn't know what to do about it. Whether you'd want me. Whether you could love me, too.'

Her eyes filled with tears. 'Of course I want you. That was the point. A fling wasn't enough. I want you for ever—because I love you, too.'

He stood up and drew her into his arms. And finally he got to do what he'd been wanting to do since the moment she'd arrived on his doorstep. He kissed her. And it felt as if something had cracked around his heart and let the sunshine back in after a long, lonely winter.

'Mr Beresford? It's Jocelyn Fisher. You left a message asking us to call you about Barrington Manor,' a plummy voice informed him later that afternoon.

'Would you mind if I put you on speakerphone?' he asked. 'Mariana Thackeray needs to hear this, too.'

'Mariana Thackeray from *Hidden Treasure*?'

'Yes.'

'How thrilling! So this is all about a painting?'

'It is,' Angelo confirmed, and explained about *The Girl in the Window*. 'So we were rather hoping that you might have some information to fill in the gaps for us,' he said. 'If you have any information about Alice, we'd love to hear it.'

'Alice's branch of the family were pretty much wiped out—the ones who survived the Great War died in the 1918 flu epidemic,' Jocelyn said. 'My husband's grandfather inherited the manor from them. His father was probably the one renovating it when your grandfather came to Barrington—the roof had a leak, and it made sense to fix it in the summer when it was more likely to be dry and you'd have longer working days. That's why they were turning out the attic and found the painting. We sold the place twenty years ago because our children didn't want the drag out to rural Norfolk—their lives are all in London, so we moved as well. We've still got fields around us, but at least now we're only an hour from the city. We still have all the family papers, though. Would you like to see them?'

'We'd love to,' Mariana said.

'When would you like to come?'

Angelo looked at Mariana and mouthed, *Tomorrow?* At her nod, he asked, 'Is tomorrow too early? Just that we're dying to fill in the gaps. Plus my grandfather's not in the best of health and I want to make as much progress as I can while he's—' He steeled himself. 'While he's still able to hear the story.'

'Oh, absolutely. I would, too, in your shoes. I'll have a rummage and see what I can dredge out. Which years are you looking at, again?'

'1862 and 1863 are the key ones,' Mariana said. 'Any mention of Domenico Carulli and Alice.'

'Right. I'll see what we have.' She gave them the address. 'I'll see you tomorrow. About ten?'

'That's perfect. Thank you. Would you like me to email over a photograph of the painting and the sketch of the woman we think is Alice?'

'That would be fabulous. Yes, please.' She

gave them her email address. 'I look forward to meeting you both.'

'Let's hope the last bit of the puzzle is in her papers,' Mariana said. 'I'd like to know if our theory was right.'

'And that Alice and Robert were happy together,' Angelo added. 'As I hope we'll be.' He paused. 'So. We're officially together.'

She smiled. 'We are indeed.'

'You've met Nonno, but I'd like to introduce you to Mamma, Cammie, Ed and Serafina.'

'You need to meet my family, too.' She looked at him. 'Today's Wednesday. It's my evening with Olly. Maybe I could ring Sophie and change it slightly—if you'd like to meet everyone tonight?'

'I'd love that,' he said. 'And perhaps you could meet everyone in Florence at the weekend.'

'That'd be wonderful,' she said.

Sophie was more than happy to change the evening's plans when Mariana video-called her. 'Whatever Mum and Dad are doing, they won't mind moving it for you. I can't believe you're… Well. You look happier than I've seen you in a very long time.'

'I am,' Mariana said softly.

'I have to admit I'm a bit nervous,' Angelo said when they went to her sister's house later that evening. 'I've worked on multi-million-pound mergers, but meeting your family feels a lot more daunting.'

'Just be yourself,' she said with a smile.

Olly opened the door to them. 'Auntie Mari! Mum, Mum, Auntie Mari's here!' He gave her a massive hug, then looked at Angelo and bit his lip.

Angelo, guessing that either the boy had been told not to talk to strangers or he was wary because Eric hadn't been very child-friendly, crouched down. 'Hello. My name's Angelo, and I'm your auntie's friend.'

The little boy looked to Mariana for guidance, and she nodded, miming a handshake.

Olly put his hand out to shake Angelo's. 'Hello,' he said. Then he frowned. 'Angelo's a funny name.'

'That's because it's an Italian name. I'm half-

Italian,' Angelo explained. 'And your auntie tells me that you love stories about my country.' He produced a book from his pocket. 'And she tells me this is the next book in the series you're reading. Perhaps I can read a bit of the first chapter with you?'

'Cool!' Olly said, grinning. Then his face fell as he remembered his manners. 'I mean, thank you.'

Angelo grinned. '"Cool" is fine by me.'

He'd brought flowers, wine and chocolates for Sophie and Laurence, but managed about three sentences before Olly talked him into reading a bit of the new story and building a complicated train set instead of chatting in the kitchen with all the adults.

'And,' Olly continued, 'I know some great jokes.'

'I know. Mariana showed me the one you sent her about the cow,' Angelo said.

'That's my favourite joke ever.' Olly grinned. 'What does a cow with no lips say?'

And he fell into peals of laughter when Angelo grinned back and said, 'Oo!'

'You've unleashed a monster now,' Sophie said, but she was laughing, too.

Mariana noticed how patient Angelo was as they read the story, helping Olly when he stumbled over an unfamiliar word, and then not minding kneeling on the floor in his expensive suit to build the train set. He didn't mind Lily, their rescue Jack Russell, washing his face and then curling up on his lap, either.

He was still every inch the clever, formal lawyer; but it was overlaid by a softer side, one she really liked. Even if they didn't manage to adopt or foster children, she thought, he was going to be a brilliant uncle. Olly already adored him.

'So you got together because of your grandfather's painting?' Carol, Mariana's mother, asked over dinner.

'It's a very special painting,' Angelo said. 'And Mariana was the only person who could find out the truth behind it.'

'My assistant was quite helpful, though,' she said, nudging him and smiling.

He slid his arm round her shoulders. 'I've

learned more than I ever knew was possible about art, over the last few weeks. My grandfather says there's hope for me yet and Mariana will reform me from being a philistine and I'll learn to appreciate paintings.'

'So what's the story behind the painting, and are you using it in the next series?' Philip, Mariana's father, asked.

Between them, Mariana and Angelo told the story behind *The Girl in the Window*.

'We're meeting the previous owners of Barrington Manor tomorrow, and we're really hoping there's a bit more behind the story,' Angelo said. His eyes crinkled at the corners as he looked at Mariana. 'I want a happy ending.'

'Absolutely,' Mariana agreed.

When they cleared the table, Carol gave Mariana a hug. 'I like him,' she said softly. 'I like the way he looks at you. He sees you for who you are, appreciates you properly.'

'He makes me feel I'm worth something,' Mariana said. 'He's the opposite of Eric. We're a team.' She smiled at her mother. 'We both want the same thing—an equal partnership.'

'Just the way it should be,' Carol declared.

'But you said he didn't want children. The way he was with Olly—that's not a man who doesn't like kids.'

'I got the wrong end of the stick,' Mariana said quietly. 'He wants kids, but he had mumps when he was young.'

'Ah. Poor man.'

'But even if our options don't work out,' she said, 'we'll have each other. And that's enough.'

'I like your family. A lot,' Angelo said to Mariana when he drove her back to her house.

'They liked you, too,' she said. 'Mum noticed the way you look at me.'

'Is that a good thing?' he asked.

'A very good thing,' she confirmed. 'You were good with Lily, too.'

'I'd like a dog,' he said.

She laughed. 'And a neat freak like you would cope with all the hair a dog sheds, and mud all over the kitchen floor?'

'There's a little thing called a vacuum cleaner. Rumour has it you can use it even if you have a Y chromosome,' he said. 'So, to answer your question, yes.'

She grinned. 'I'll hold you to that. Even though I know you have a cleaner.'

'A house can still be a home if it's tidy,' he said. 'The important thing is that it's filled with love. And respect.'

'And paintings. Absolutely.' She kissed him. 'I hope you weren't planning on going home until after breakfast.'

'I hope,' he said, 'that was an invitation.'

'It is,' she confirmed, and led him inside.

The next morning, they stopped at Angelo's house so he could change his clothes, then he drove them to Chigwell to meet the Fishers.

'The last piece of the puzzle,' Angelo said as he parked the car. 'I hope.'

Mariana rang the doorbell, and a slender woman with white hair opened the door.

'You must be Angelo and Miss Thackeray,' she said.

'Please, call me Mariana,' Mariana said.

'And I'm Jocelyn.' She shook their hands warmly. 'Come in, come in.' Two black and white springer spaniels bounced around at her heels; Jocelyn shushed them and sent them back to their beds, then led Mariana and Angelo through a red-tiled hallway to the kitchen containing an Aga and a scrubbed pine kitchen table, where she made them all some very strong coffee.

'Keith—my husband—is away, but he'll be thrilled to know about it when he gets back. I had a rummage through what he likes to call the archives—we probably shouldn't keep them in the cellar and ought to deposit them in the Records Office, but you know *men*.' She rolled her eyes. 'Anyway. I've found an awful lot. It's terribly exciting—almost like being on one of those genealogy shows and discovering things about relatives you had no idea about.'

'We're featuring the painting on *Hidden Treasure*, so there's a chance you could be on the show,' Mariana said.

'Well, not me—it ought to be Keith, really, as he's the Fisher. And obviously I realise it's all terribly confidential. Come and see what I found. Bring your coffee.'

The spaniels pattered behind them as Jocelyn led them to the dining room; the table was easily big enough to seat twelve, and there were papers stacked neatly across it.

'Charles Fisher—he must be a cousin or some kind of great-uncle to Keith, though I haven't sat down and worked it out properly—owned the house in 1862. In 1863 the household account book shows a payment to a drawing master.' She opened the book with a flourish. Next to a modern index tab marking the right place on the page, in neat Victorian copperplate, were the words *Drawing Master, Domenico Carulli.*

'There's some paperwork here, too. It seems Carulli was allowed to stay in one of the farm cottages on New Road.'

'That ties up with the letter he wrote his brother,' Angelo said.

'Now, Harriet Fisher—Charles's wife—kept a diary. Her writing's terribly cramped and it took me ages to work it out, but it seems this Domenico Carulli painted matching portraits of Harriet and Charles in 1862 in return for being allowed to staying at one of the cottages and paint landscapes over the summer.'

'That's wonderful,' Angelo said. 'Do you still have the paintings?'

'Sadly not,' Jocelyn said. 'But we do have some sketches.'

There were sketches of a man and a woman, both signed; the back of the sketches held their names and the date, June 1862.

'They're both very fashionably dressed,' Mariana said. 'And, although I'm guessing you'd never want to sell them, Angelo's grand-father's gallery might ask if they can borrow them from time to time for an exhibition.'

'I'm sure we can arrange something,' Jocelyn said with a smile. 'I photocopied these for you, and the diary, because I think you'll find them interesting. Now, we also had a photographer at the house who came from London—you know they did these *cartes de visite* thingies?'

'There was a real craze for them in the eighteen-sixties,' Mariana said. Angelo looked blank, so she explained, 'They were paper prints mounted on thin card, the same size as a calling card. They were the first cheaply available portraits, and as well as taking por-traits of ordinary people, photographers sold portraits of Queen Victoria and Dickens and other celebrities of the day. People used to collect them and put them in an album.'

'That's what they did at Barrington,' Jocelyn said. 'Everyone in the house had one done, somewhere around the summer of 1861. And I mean everyone, including the servants and the labourers on the farm—at some point someone's put them neatly in an album. I don't know who, as it's not the same handwriting as Harriet's.'

She showed them a small leather-bound album, not much larger than the size of a *carte de visite*, which had a spring-loaded clasp. She unclipped it to reveal the pages inside; each had a square mount and a slot underneath it where the *carte de visite* was slid into the album and underneath the slot was a small box where someone had written in names in copperplate handwriting.

'The first one, of course, was Charles.' The full-length photograph showed a rather stern-looking man—the man from the sketch Jocelyn had shown them earlier. 'And Harriet.' Again, she was the image of the sketch they'd seen. 'But this is the one I think you'll really like.' She skipped over a couple of pages. 'Meet Alice Fisher.'

The photograph matched the sketch and the portrait in oils, albeit in the photograph Alice was clearly a couple of years younger—and that tied up, too.

'*The Girl in the Window*. She's definitely Alice. You've just given us the final bit of proof to tie them all together. Thank you so much!' Mariana said, and threw her arms round Jocelyn.

Then she turned to Angelo and hugged him, too. 'We've done it. We can prove your grandfather's painting is a Carulli.'

Thanks to Mariana's persistence, they'd beaten the ticking clock. His grandfather still wouldn't be with them at Christmas, but Leo would die happy, knowing that he'd been right about his painting.

Angelo held her close, unable to speak and hoping that she'd understand how overwhelmed he felt right at that moment.

'The story gets a lot more interesting,' Jocelyn said with a grin. 'You wait until you see

Harriet's diary. I'm guessing Charles didn't know about it—it's in tiny handwriting, and in a tiny, tiny book, a bit like Jane Austen writing her novels on tiny sheets of paper she could hide easily. I took a photocopy for you, but obviously we can make the original available if you need it.'

'That's amazing,' Angelo said. 'Really wonderful. Thank you.'

A mobile phone shrilled, and Jocelyn groaned. 'Sorry, I'm expecting this and I really have to take it. It's my granddaughter, having wedding panics, and she's fighting with my daughter, and I need to go and smooth all the ruffled feathers. Can I leave you to look at the diary on your own?'

'Of course,' Angelo said.

'Sweetie? Yes, I'm here,' Jocelyn said, blew them a kiss and left the room.

Mariana looked at Angelo. 'It seems a bit unfair, reading this without Jocelyn.'

'She suggested we look at it,' Angelo reminded her. 'I vote we start at June 1863.'

'Agreed,' she said.

They flipped through the photocopied sheets until they found the right date.

'Jocelyn wasn't kidding. Harriet's writing is minuscule,' Angelo said.

They pored over the sheets of paper, and because the handwriting was so small they were forced to move closer together. Angelo couldn't resist sliding his arm round her.

'We're meant to be working,' Mariana said, but the sternness in her voice was completely fake and totally undercut by the gleam in her eye.

'Of course we're working. It's just more comfortable like this.' Angelo drew her a tiny bit closer to him.

'You might be right,' Mariana said, and her smile made his heart feel as if it had just done a somersault.

They turned back to the diary. 'Here's Signor Carulli arriving again, in June,' Angelo said.

'He's engaged as the drawing master, and Alice's sketching is coming on well. Her father's pleased with her accomplishments and he's planning to marry her off to the son of one of their neighbours,' Mariana said.

There was nothing of real note during the rest of June and July. Then Angelo frowned. 'Look at this one in August. *"Alice has been pale every morning,"'* he read. '*"I fear she has ceased to be unwell."* Does that mean she'd stopped having morning sickness?'

'No, it means she's stopped menstruating,' Mariana said. 'See here, on the next page. *"I fear she is in a delicate condition."* Harriet obviously thinks Alice is pregnant.' Even saying the word made her feel guilty. This must be so hard for Angelo, reading about a pregnancy, when his marriage had broken down because of his infertility.

The next page was heartbreaking. 'Poor Alice,' Mariana said. 'She really got swept off her feet by Carulli. A lot of models fell for their painters. And here she's obviously confessed to her mother. *"She told me she posed for him…one thing led to another."* Poor Alice. That must've been so hard for her. She must've been terrified of being thrown out and left to deal with everything alone.' She grimaced. 'And it wasn't just the scandal. In Victorian times, pregnancy was dangerous. Women died in childbirth—and so did the babies. Harriet had seven children that we know of, so she knew the risks.'

'But Harriet's definitely on her side. *"I have told Charles. He was going to horsewhip the drawing master from here to Norwich. I persuaded him not to,"*' Angelo read.

'Adding scandal to scandal. Pregnant by someone who wasn't only from a different class, he was from a different country. If Charles beat him up, it would just confirm the gossip and make things harder for Alice,' Mariana said.

'Now it's September, and Carulli's left. And here's Harriet worrying again. *"She does not show. I could send Alice to my sister in Scotland, until after."*' Angelo frowned again. 'You mean she's actually thinking of letting Alice have the baby but then taking it away from her?'

'To be brought up by someone else—it's one possible solution,' Mariana said. 'Look here— she says she could go with Alice and they could come back and say the baby belonged to Harriet and Charles.' She paused. 'Except the servants, especially the ones who did the laundry, would know that Harriet showed no sign of pregnancy and Alice did.'

A week later there was another entry. *'"Charles says it is settled. She will marry Robert Reynolds, his tenant at Manor Farm,"'* Angelo read. *'"Charles will settle the farm on Reynolds, provided the baby is his heir."* We were right, then. It was a marriage of convenience.'

'Harriet's heartbroken about it, though,' Mariana said. 'Not because of the scandal, but because she's afraid Alice will be unhappy. *"My poor Alice. He is so much older than she is. But Charles is adamant. If we go to Scotland he will make us come back. He will not say that the baby is ours."'*

'And that would add to the shame,' Angelo said with a sigh. 'Look, there's another entry here. Charles has paid for the licence and the wedding is set for the first of October.'

'There's nothing in here about how Alice felt. But I guess she was trapped,' Mariana said. 'Carulli had gone back to Italy, and he might've confessed to her beforehand that he was married. Her only option was to have the baby and brazen it out.'

They pored over the diary again. 'Harriet doesn't say much about the wedding,' Mariana said thoughtfully. 'Just *"It is done. Alice is married to Reynolds"*. Instead of being the big society event, consolidating the relationship with another landowning family like they'd planned, it's a quick and quiet wedding.'

'Let's see if there's anything about the baby,' Angelo said. 'I need to know that she loved the baby.'

She knew what was getting to him, and reached up to kiss him. 'It's going to be all right,' she said softly. And she didn't just mean Alice. 'Here we go. March. *"Alice has been delivered safely of a boy. People will count on their fingers and talk, but no matter. Robert will stand up for her."'* She paused. 'I notice Harriet calls him by his first name now. I think she likes him.'

'"Alice has been teaching Robert to write,"' Angelo read. 'So they're managing to rub along.'

'Even though he isn't the man she fell in love

with, the father of her baby, it sounds as if she's happy,' Mariana said. 'I'm glad.'

'I'm glad, too. Though I wish we knew more. Carulli said to his brother that he left under a cloud, so it's obvious he knew about the baby. But was Alice just an idle fling or did he really love her? And did he really just walk away from a baby?'

She stroked his face. 'I'm sorry. This must be so hard for you.'

'It is. I know, I know, he was already married to someone in Florence and had children with her, so technically he couldn't marry Alice, but how could he just walk out on his child? How could he walk out on any of them?' He shook his head. 'Even if you allow for infant mortality being high and parents being too scared to love their babies too much in case they lost them—that's *cold.*'

Before she could say anything to reassure him, Jocelyn bustled back in to the dining room. 'Sorry about that. All feathers smoothed over.'

'That's good,' Mariana said brightly. 'I'm afraid we were a bit bad and skimmed the diary for the relevant dates rather than reading it properly.'

'So we know now our theory was right.' Angelo paused. 'Did you read on after Thomas's birth?'

'I did.' Jocelyn said. 'There's nothing more about the painter. He's not a relative of yours, is he?'

'No. Just my grandfather likes his work and collected it,' Angelo said.

'I think Carulli was a total bastard, seducing her and abandoning her like that. But I guess you can like the art without liking the artist,' Jocelyn mused.

'It's a shame Carulli didn't try to do the right thing by Alice,' Mariana said. 'But it seems she was happy with Robert.'

'Oh, she was. I think they had a good life. Did you see, she taught him to read and write? I think she made the best of it. And I think they were happy. Keith says there's a lovely monument to her in the church. I'll have a look through the rest of the papers, though. See if there are any letters or anything,' Jocelyn promised.

'My producer is going to love the story,' Mariana said. 'So I'm pretty sure he's going to ask to film some of your records.'

'For a story with a happy ending? That'd be terrific,' Jocelyn said. 'Keith will be thrilled, too.'

'We've got the truth now,' Mariana said as Angelo drove them back to London. 'And enough proof to say that the painting is definitely by Carulli. Your grandfather is going to be so happy when we tell him.'

'I think,' Angelo said, 'he's going to be a lot happier about something else.' He smiled. 'About you and me.'

On Saturday morning, when they reached the *palazzo*, Angelo's mother and sister greeted Mariana with effusive hugs.

'We love your show,' Camilla said.

'And how wonderful that you've found out the truth about Babbo's painting,' Lucrezia said.

'My producer's absolutely thrilled, and so is my supervisor at the university,' Mariana said with a smile. 'Though I couldn't have done it without Angelo.'

'I couldn't have done it without you,' Angelo said. 'Teamwork.'

'That's a good thing, teamwork. Like I had with my Frederica,' Leo said.

'It's important for a happy relationship,' Lucrezia said. 'You don't have to be the same. Your father and I were opposites in many ways, Angelo. But we always worked together.'

'It's the same with my parents,' Mariana said. 'They've been married for forty years and they still hold hands.' She smiled at Camilla. 'And I've been looking forward to meeting Serafina. Angelo tells me he fell in love with her the second he held her.'

Camilla's eyes widened.

'She knows everything,' Angelo said softly. 'And it's fine.'

'It might not always be easy, but it'll be fine,' Mariana agreed.

Camilla blinked back the tears. 'That's… That's good to know.'

'I hope you don't mind, but I saw this beautiful soft rabbit—just like one I bought my nephew when he was born—and I thought Serafina might like it,' Mariana said.

'You can never have too many toys,' Cammie said, accepting the gift. 'Thank you. Would you like a cuddle with the baby?'

'I'd love one.' She cradled the baby tenderly, and seeing her like that gave Angelo a jolt. She looked so *right*. After Stephanie had left him, he'd thought that it wouldn't be possible for him to make a family. And yet when Mariana looked up and caught his gaze, he knew that she was thinking the same thing. That it wasn't going to be quick or easy, but they'd support each other and eventually they'd get their dream.

'Come and sit down and tell me about my *Girl*,' Leo said.

They retired to the Red Room; Mariana sat on the sofa, cuddling the baby, and Angelo sat beside her.

'It took us a while to piece the story together,' Mariana said. 'But it starts in 1862, when Carulli painted the portraits of the owner of Barrington Manor, Charles Fisher, and his wife Harriet. The following summer, he was taken on as the drawing master to their younger children—including Alice, their seventeen-year-old daughter.'

'Carulli and Alice fell in love,' Angelo said, 'and by September it was clear that Alice was pregnant. But Carulli was already married, with two small children and a baby, so he couldn't marry her.'

'He wrote to his brother that he had to leave England under a cloud,' Mariana said. 'We think that's when Alice's parents found out she was pregnant. Alice's father insisted that Alice had to marry Robert Reynolds, the tenant farmer who lived at Manor Farm.'

'The house in my painting,' Leo said.

'Exactly. We think Charles gave him the farm for marrying Alice and saving her from scandal,' Angelo said. 'Except it wasn't a loveless marriage. From what we can see in Harriet's diary, Alice taught Robert to read, and she had baby Thomas in 1864. We know from Robert's four-times great-granddaughter that they both died at the farm from old age and Thomas inherited the farm, and from Alice's family on the other side that there's a beautiful memorial to her in the church.'

'We've got a photograph of Alice—a *carte de visite*—from 1861, and one of Robert. That came from the Fisher side of the family,' Mariana said. 'Alice's family died in the 1918 flu epidemic, and the branch who inherited it and met you when they found the painting, Leo, kept all the paperwork. That's how we know about Harriet's diary. Jocelyn made a copy for us and we've done one for you, Leo.'

'So why was the painting in the attic?' Camilla asked.

'Our theory is that Carulli accidentally left it behind when he went back to Italy, and the Fishers found it in his cottage. They recognised their daughter but they couldn't have the painting on show because it was a reminder of the man who painted it—the man who brought shame on them,' Angelo said. 'But they loved Alice and it was a good painting, so they couldn't bring themselves to throw it away.'

'My guess is that Harriet hid the painting in the attic, and didn't tell anyone about it. When she died, nobody knew it was there, and it stayed hidden in the attic until there was a leak in the roof and the attic had to be emptied so it could be fixed,' Mariana said.

'Which is when it got eaten by the mice and you saw it, Babbo,' Lucrezia said. 'Yes, it all makes sense.'

'So is it going to be in your programme, Mariana?' Leo asked.

'Absolutely. And I think when you set up your gallery, we could do a display about the story behind the painting, with copies of the photographs and Harriet's diary, plus the studies we found of Alice and the farmhouse,' Mariana said.

'But did Carulli ever acknowledge the baby?' Camilla asked. 'It seems so heartless just to— well, walk away and abandon Alice like that.'

'He didn't have a choice,' Mariana said. 'But I'm hoping there might be something more in Jocelyn's archives, another diary entry perhaps or a letter. She's promised to let us know if she finds anything, and Angelo and I are going to check through the archives for the later letters Carulli wrote.'

'So we have definite proof, Nonno, that you

were right about the painting all along,' Angelo said.

'My *Girl*,' Leo said, smiling.

Later that evening, Angelo and Mariana went for a stroll down to the Ponte Vecchio; they stood under the arches in the centre of the bridge, watching the sky streaked with pink and orange and gold reflected in the water.

'So we found the truth about Nonno's painting—and now he knows. He's happy,' Angelo said. 'Thank you.'

'It was my job,' Mariana said. 'Though I should tell you now that I'm not accepting payment for it.'

He coughed. 'You're under contract. You have to accept payment.'

'Maybe I'll lose the paperwork.'

'Maybe I have copies.'

She grinned. 'Knowing you, it'll be in triplicate and filed away neatly. I don't care. You're not paying me for this, Angelo.'

'There's only one way I'll agree to that,' he said softly. 'And that's if you do it for love. As part of my family.'

She stared at him, her eyes wide. 'Are you...?'

'As a lawyer, perhaps I should clarify that,' he said.

She could hardly breathe; she simply nodded.

'I love you, Mariana. And in discovering the truth behind Nonno's painting I've discovered the truth about what I really want from life—to spend my days with you and, if we're lucky, our children. But even if we don't have children, we'll still be lucky because we have each other.' He dropped down to one knee. 'Will you marry me?'

There was only one answer she could make.

'I love you, too. Yes.'

Angelo stood up again, smiling. 'As a lawyer, I should ask for consideration to seal a contract.'

'Consideration?'

He drew her into his arms. 'A kiss. Our first kiss as an engaged couple.'

'That sounds perfect to me.' She smiled, and kissed him.

EPILOGUE

Two years later

'OPENING NIGHT,' ANGELO SAID, his arm round Mariana's shoulders as they strolled through the rooms. 'It feels odd that the *palazzo*'s a gallery now—after all these years when it was Nonno's home.'

'But you've done a brilliant job setting it up,' she said. 'He'd be so proud of you.'

'And of you. The way you put the exhibition together, with all those parts to the story of *The Girl in the Window*. I wish he was here to see it,' Angelo said.

'But he knew the truth about the painting before he died. That we had proof it was by Carulli, that all the tests came back and said it was definitely his work. And he knew that Carulli didn't abandon Alice completely—he wrote to Harriet and he sent money for the baby. And he told her he loved Alice, and he knew it was wrong to fall in love with her as well as his wife, but he couldn't help it.' The letters Jocelyn had found among the family papers had given them all some closure: the artist hadn't been completely heartless.

'And Nonno was able to take part in the filming of the episode,' Angelo said. 'Award-winning episode, as of last month, I should say,' he corrected. 'Well, Dr Beresford. I think we should have a private glass of champagne before the rest of the family gets here and before we open the doors.'

'Half a glass,' she said. 'Because this week isn't just the opening of the Leo Moretti gallery.'

It was also the week their IVF treatment was going to start.

'There's only a twenty-five per cent chance that it will work,' he warned.

'But, if it doesn't, we have other options,' she said. 'And, most importantly, we have each other. We always will.'

He kissed her. 'I love you, my clever, talented, wonderful wife with the biggest heart in the world. I still can't believe you dedicated your doctoral thesis to Nonno.'

'Of course I did. His collection made a massive difference to what I wrote.'

'I love you,' he said again.

She grinned. 'Even though I've made you put paintings in every single room of your house?'

'*Our* house,' he corrected. 'Yes.'

'Good. I love you, too.'

He opened a bottle of champagne and poured two half-glasses. 'To Carulli,' he said, 'who didn't exactly behave well, but without him you and I would never have had an excuse to meet.'

'And to Nonno,' she said, 'who found the painting.'

'And to us,' he said, 'for daring to be brave.' He kissed her again. 'I love you. Always.'

* * * * *

LET'S TALK

Romance

For exclusive extracts, competitions
and special offers, find us online:

f facebook.com/millsandboon

📷 @millsandboonuk

🐦 @millsandboon

Or get in touch on 0844 844 1351*

For all the latest titles coming soon,
visit millsandboon.co.uk/nextmonth